CELESTIAL LIAISON

The Cavanaugh Series

JC Wardon

A Mystic Waters Book

Mystic Waters Books
JC Wardon

CELESTIAL LIAISON
Copyright © 2016, JC Wardon
Trade Paperback ISBN: 978-1-944454-70-8

Editor, Gilly Wright
Cover Art Design by Calliope-Designs.com

Digital Release, 2015
Trade Paperback Release, March 2016

Media > Books > Fiction > Romance Novels
Keywords: romance, paranormal, angel, witch, shapeshifter

This print edition is published by author/owner JC Wardon, Mystic Waters Books

JC Wardon
www.jcwardon.com

CELESTIAL LIAISON

What's a woman to do when the Angel of Death comes knocking at her heart?

Celestia Cavanaugh Hansen is ready for her life to begin. She thinks her mystical gift may finally be manifesting, and she's starting up the veterinary practice of her dreams. But when a stranger lands on her parent's mountain property as if having fallen from the sky, she finds herself smitten and finds her heart, too, is coming to life.

In order to reclaim his place in the ANGELIC REALM, Sabian must redeem himself after failing to claim a soul. Even though his angelic powers were stripped away, as well as the title by which he'd always been known, the former ANGEL OF DEATH now has to fix what he messed up, and do it as nothing more than a human male. Which means he must take the life of another...

Chapter One

"You have only two choices. Obedience or dissolution.

"Should you wish to continue existing, you may resume seeking the Foretold human female, as was your charge. All previous duties are no longer yours, most particularly that which you intentionally undertook—and subsequently failed at. This disobedience on top of the others has placed not only you, but all in peril. As I'm told is your habit, you did not take your new duty seriously enough to follow it through. Instead of being thankful for a new assignment rather than the elimination you deserved, you once again chose your own path.

"We do not do this!"

Sabian winced at the unexpected shout from Riagan Absalom, but said nothing.

"It is only because we have a forgiving Creator that you are again blessed and given yet another chance to redeem yourself. Go forward now, and do what you were to do before. The Foretold One, alone, can open the door for our army to emerge as the time of Blood Moon approaches. If you succeed this time, perhaps you can redeem yourself in the eyes of The Creator.

"This. Is. Your. Last. Chance. Fail again, your spirit will dissolve and you will have never been."

Sabian remained prostrate on the Third-Heaven cloud, just outside what humankind called the pearly gates. His face bathed in the cool mist as fear and anger radiating from his pores for all those witnessing to sense and smell. He'd made a big mistake. He became distracted from his reassignment, by the dying body lying so close to where he'd been on his actual mission. And an even bigger gaffe when he'd taken her soul only to lose it to something he still did not understand. But he's always gone his own way, and the urge to reap a soul, even though he no longer had that right, had been instinctual. *To lose it though,* after already disobeying, was the greatest of all his sins. The problem was he had no way to explain to himself what had happened when her soul had been pulled from heaven and returned to earth abruptly, much less to those to whom he answered. Not that excuses were accepted.

Ever!

"The one you were to seek is still located where she was on the earth, as is the one whose body you failed to deliver. The Foretold comes from a family gifted with powers many generations past, and because all but a few used them as intended for three millennia—for the good of mankind—their gifts continue to this day. This is something you could learn from."

"I don't understand."

With twisted lips, Riagan Absalom shook his head. "It is not your place to understand, only to do as you are told. We are servants of the Master and nothing more. That, too, is something you would do well to remember.

"Now you have two charges: to acquire the one for the greater purpose, as you were commissioned to do, and to attain the soul of the other. Her soul was neither hers to keep nor yours to lose in the first place. Successfully completing both tasks may be your only salvation should you chose to take on these quests."

Sabian glanced up. "How am I to complete this task with no knowledge of how to do so?"

"I only tell you what came from the Master's mouth to Michael, and from him to me, to pass forward to you. Pay close attention.

"It is your choice how to complete these tasks. That, in itself, is a test of your worthiness. You will find this woman by her blood, and then you must get the chosen one to agree to leave the life she knows. But she must come to aid us of her own free will. You must also now take the life of the other so her soul will abide where it was meant to go when she died. You are never to reveal your true self to either once you realize who you really are. The Almighty knows all and will be watching you closely."

Sabian frowned. *Realize who he really is? What does that mean?* Before he could speak his questions aloud, his prosecutor continued.

"No matter what you do, the Foretold One's sacrifice must be pure and unconditional, or all will be in vain. If she is willing to give up her current life for the greater good, and you retrieve the soul you lost, you will then resume your place in the Heavenly Host. For reasons that escape me—though it is not my place to question—you will also be given back the position you so covet. If you cannot or will not accomplish these tasks as dictated, you will have never been.

"Do you accept these terms?"

Even though the terms had been reemphasized, Sabian was more confused than ever. *Now* there was a chance he'd be rewarded with his old existence, if he fell in line?

There was nothing to do, save nod. There was no choice for him to do otherwise, and the Brotherhood knew it.

It grated, though. Since the time-before-time, he'd had more freedoms than any other angel created. His job as soul-transporter following a human's death had taken him everywhere on the earth, and he'd gained more knowledge of those who roamed the little planet as a whole than even the Guardians. They only serviced one individual's lifespan at a time and had a very limited view of what people were really like. Sabian knew so much more than the Guardian Angels ever hoped to know, even more than those currently standing around to observe his degradation. It made him shake inside to keep from telling them so. The Brotherhood assembled here knew nothing about the humans, except for their need to find those human women with the silver blood.

It infuriated Sabian further, that he'd served his original purpose well since the time-before-time, and *still* he was demoted to the equivalent of what humans called an errand-boy, over the few previous months. His freedoms had been lost, his tasks made mundane, and his movements were monitored and restricted.

It was true he'd taken advantage of the freedom to roam the human world since the beginning. He hadn't realized his sins had been tallied-up and judged. He knew now he should have just accepted his demotion, but accepting less than he wanted had never been his way. Now he'd blown it big-time by doing the unthinkable. Not only had he overstepped and disobeyed a direct order, he'd lost a soul that was never his to retrieve to start with.

But old habits die hard, as the humans would say.

"There is one last thing…"

Sabian raised his head again to look at Riagan Absalom, the reigning Prince of The Brotherhood of the Repentant. The prince's beauty radiated like a starburst around him, his purity of spirit painful to behold. It vexed Sabian that Riagan had been elevated to a position above

Sabian's own. A wisp of angst filled him as well, and Sabian recognized it for the jealousy it was.

"And what is that?" Sabian asked, his disdain unintentionally obvious.

Humor filled the prince's eyes, but he spoke with a seriousness that bespoke his sadness. "Once you are upon the earth, you will no longer have your angelic supremacies, nor will you be able to think of yourself, or speak of yourself, with your angelic appellation. You will, in fact, have no knowledge of your past, until the day the Foretold is revealed to you.

"At that time you will regain your memories and your name, Sabian, Reaper of the Dead. But, until you have succeeded in these quests and are fully redeemed in the eyes of The Creator, you are *Oublié le Dechu*."

Forgotten, the Fallen....

Sabian winced, as everything within him shook uncontrollably. "And by what name am I to be called by the humans?"

The prince slid a glance to the others present, seemingly unaware his words were shattering Sabian into pieces. He returned his gaze upon Sabian, as a less than angelic smile touching his lips.

"You will know yourself as Sabastian Envoi. The first, because it has no meaning to us other than it is your name, but more. The second, because it is your charge to travel to earth and liaise with The Foretold, to fulfil both her destiny and your own."

Looking annoyed, Riagan continued. "You will lose your angelic face and form, as well as your memories until the time of reaping has come. You will take on the features and the weaknesses of mankind. Though you will be granted the knowledge common to that of a man of five-and-twenty earthy years, you will receive a mind of pureness as if a newly born babe. Once memories do return, you will have nothing more than your powers of persuasion to accomplish your goal with the Foretold. As to the other..." Riagan shook his head as his eyes lost their luster and held bewilderment. "It is up to you how and when you take her physical life, but it must be before you have secured—and delivered—the Foretold."

Sabian looked around. With the exception of the prince, all angelic heads bowed as though none could bear to look upon him. He felt the silent condemnation of each, something he'd never expected possible. Destitute of spirit, Sabian said not a word. It wasn't in him to ask how they expected him to take a life, when such was never a celestial's charge. The soul, yes—by a reaper alone, just as he'd once been. But only once a life ended. Never the life itself.

What sounded like the prince clearing his throat caused Sabian to turn back to him. "Am I done here?" Sabian asked, angry fear twisting his midsection.

There was chiding in Riagan Absalom's eyes as he shook his head. "There is more.

"No Celestials upon earth or here shall recognize you in your new form, save for the Master Himself. And you cannot identify yourself to those of us who may be near, should you detect our presence once you are again yourself. If you do attempt to do so, you will immediately be nothing but a memory soon wiped clean from our minds. In essence, Sabian, former Reaper of the Dead, you are *on your own* from this time forward."

The assembled Brotherhood of the Repentant took a collective breath. The punishment was harsh indeed. Sabian heard another collective gasp when the prince raised a hand, and what held his own angelic form aloft disappeared.

Feeling the rush of wind as he dropped through the clouds was stunning. The spinning, which soon started and increased with the downward thrust, built to such a speed it became endlessly terrifying. He landed on his feet what seemed eons later, but an abrupt, jarring, end-of-motion spear of spiraling pain dashed upward through the center of his body and took him down onto his hands and knees. The sounds that fled up his throat and out his mouth were new to him, as was the agony he felt at landing on cold hard ground that threw up white ice. He struggled for breath through the pain, his mind bombarded with sensations he'd never before experienced. At least he didn't think so....

Panicked that he couldn't breathe or think clearly, since the oxygen in his brain was depleting, he clawed at his throat. His entire body clenched, shuddered, and seized, until finally, blessedly, his lungs filled with crisp air.

Relieved tears streamed down his face, their warmth a sharp contrast to his chilled cheeks. Afraid to move more than his head, he surveyed the white powder-coated bases of the many trees around him. It took several minutes for the shock to settle in his bones. Since he'd landed in snow and was as naked as a newly born baby, he feared the tremors were turning to chills he had no way of curtailing. There was a steady ice-cold breeze, blowing more white crystal flakes around the trees and his limbs.

A curse was on the tip of his lips, but something within him held it there. He swallowed and struggled to rise. He tried to ignore his stinging palms, knees, and the blood that surely seeped from the soles of his feet. He hit his hands against each other, and then swiped at his knees to knock away the bloody powdered snow and imbedded twigs lodged there. He glanced on down to find his toes as bloody red as the snow beneath them. They tingled with sharp pain, the tips already turning a strange shade. He lifted a leg and knocked the snow from one foot, only to lose his balance. Thankful he caught himself before landing on his already aching hip, he looked around for somewhere to hide from the wind and stumbled over to settle at the rough base of a thick pine.

Every part of him shivered. Every inch screamed with pain. He settled his bare bottom against the rough bark and cried out as it scratched his already frozen buttocks. Tears again stung his eyes as he collapsed into as tight a ball as he could, but nothing eased the painful cold or the realization he was somehow in a forest and had no memory of how he came to be there.

Fear flooded his chest as the thought brought harsh laughter to his stiff lips, causing them to pull painfully. His lungs struggled to continue working even though it felt as if they stuck together between each bitterly chilled breath. His mind fought to figure out what had happened to him, rather than give in and close down. And his body, as much as it hurt, still wanted to move to keep from freezing to death. He struggled to his feet, knowing there was no way he'd survive if he didn't get going…somewhere. Each step was achingly painful, but the faster he moved, the looser his limbs got. Though he had little hope he'd keep from freezing before he found a way out of the woods, his uproarious mind told him not to go down without trying.

It seemed forever he walked, ran, stumbled, and forced himself to keep going. His entire body was a pain-absorbing, heavy burden. His appendages felt awkward, as if new to his body, and took in the cold far too quickly. Especially the fingers, toes, and the penis dangling at the apex of his thighs.

The sounds of an oncoming vehicle cause him to stumble to a halt. At first, he wasn't sure what direction to turn. The noise of the motor seemed to bounce off the rocks from all directions. He closed his eyes and made himself take slow even breaths as he concentrated. That others were near meant his salvation might possibly be at hand. Hoping he turned in the right direction, he hurried as fast as the sharp pains in his toes would allow. The steam from each harsh breath that blew back out of his mouth and nose made him look like the running engine of a steam locomotive of decades past. He had no idea how he knew that.

He fell to his knees when he reached the edge of the cliff and saw the ribbon of road below. Though the vehicle he'd heard earlier was long gone, surely, even in the snowy conditions, someone else would soon come along.

At least he hoped so.

He took the time to rub at his arms and legs, his feet and even the toes he feared would soon be lost. He blew into his cupped palms, and danced from foot to foot to restore circulation that should have already been completely lost. He decided it didn't matter if he cursed. Or threw one hell of a fit. If he didn't find help quickly....

No sooner did the thought enter his mind, he heard the sounds of another vehicle approaching and knew capturing the attention of whoever drove was vital. He took another deep breath, this time for courage, and blew it out as he leaped, felt those few chilling seconds of the frigid wind carrying him, and landed on the road with a splat, crackle and pop.

He couldn't move and knew he shouldn't try. Which was surprising since he couldn't seem to wrap his mind around anything except the pain. And the cold. And the realization the sound of the vehicle was getting closer. And he was lying dead center in its path.

The blare of a horn was followed by the squeal of brakes and the scent of locked tires. He closed his eyes and uttered the only prayer he could think of.

"Oh, God!"

Chapter Two

Celestia pressed the plunger slowly, removed the needle and stepped back as her heart ached. Of all the things required of her chosen career, this was always the hardest to endure. It was her very first patient as the new owner of the clinic. She waited silently, trying to keep her own tears in check as Chili Pepper's owners sobbed quietly. The little Chihuahua had lived a long love-filled life, but that didn't matter to the older couple who still considered her their baby. When the wife turned and left the examining room, Celestia peered at the husband. "I'll wrap her up in her blanket, and put her in a box for you if you'd like." When Charles Stanley nodded, Celestia did as well. "Okay. Do you want her collar? Or would you like it to be with her?"

He cleared his throat and looked at her with watery eyes. "I'll take it. We have her toys and things waiting in the car. We'll put them with her later, at the cemetery."

Nodding, Celestia handed him the rhinestone-decorated strap of pink leather and waited until he left the room before she opened the little cabinet filled with the various-sized boxes needed for this sad chore. She lifted Chili Pepper gently and took her favorite blanket from beneath her. With care, she formed a little nest and curled the pup's body so she looked like she rested peacefully, then ran a gentle hand over her tiny head one last time.

Celestia swallowed against the tightness in her throat as she maneuvered the cardboard flaps so they would remain closed but allow Chili Pepper's parents to open them once they reached the pet cemetery across town. Reining in her emotions, she carried the dog to the outer room, nearly releasing a checked tear when Mrs. Stanley's sobs wracked her thin shoulders.

After handing the box to the husband, Celestia pulled the elderly woman in for a hug. "I'm so very sorry for your loss," she said, knowing they would mourn their baby for months to come. At first, the sorrow would be continuous, then over the weeks at feeding time, potty time, or out of the blue, while sitting in front of a television set. There she would have once lain in a lap or beside a thigh, just waiting for that offhanded swipe of hand to fur-covered head, a touch both pet-lover and fur-baby knew was love given and love received.

Celestia exhaled a shaky breath and went back to sanitize the stainless steel table before she locked up for the night. She was physically tired from her first full day on her own and emotionally exhausted. It always pained her to end a life, even if it was the kindest thing to do for a suffering animal. The sound of the outer door opening was the last thing she wanted to hear. Given the way the snow came down through the frosty window, she feared one of her clients must really be in bad shape for its owner to make the trip out to see her tonight.

She hurried through the examining room door and stopped short when she saw her cousin instead. Diamond Cavanaugh White looked like hell, to put it mildly, which propelled Celestia's feet faster across the tiled floor. The normally smiling blond beauty's light blue eyes were red-rimmed and filled with tears. Her clothing was usually casual but now looked rumpled as if she'd worn them to bed…for several nights.

"Dia! What's happened?"

Dia shook her head as she accepted Celestia's hug. "Nothing. Something. Everything!" Dia flung hysterically, before she began crying.

Celestia headed back to her office and quickly snagged tissues, as well as a bottle of water. She handed the tissues to Dia and waited as her cousin blew her nose. When she took the water, Dia downed half of it in one long gulp.

"You're scaring me. What's going on?"

Dia dug in her purse and pulled out an oblong white object that showed two lines across its little window. "I think I'm pregnant!"

Her first reaction was one of joy Dia finally knew, but Celestia tempered it, knowing her cousin still didn't have any idea of all that had happened to her months before. She bit her bottom lip, wondering how to handle what her elders had decided need handling another way.

"We have to call your mother."

Dia shook her head, sending her blond hair flying. "I can't. They're on a plane on the way to California."

Surprised at the news, since nothing ever happened in the family that everyone wasn't quickly aware of, she nodded. "Okay, then we'll call mine."

"We can't. All our moms and dads went. Something serious is going on with Gavin's wife and his son, and they left immediately after getting the call. They won't be there until they land around three tomorrow morning." She lifted tearful eyes and shook her head. "I don't want them to know yet."

"Dia..." Celestia was at a loss.

"I don't know how this happened!"

Still knocked off her feet by the news of the parents' flight to aid the man they considered a cousin, Celestia took Dia's hand and led her to the closest chair. "Aunt Destiny and Uncle Tom went, too?"

Dia nodded. "Yes, *all* of them."

With her palm against her forehead, Celestia nodded, realizing she'd been so busy preparing to make so many major changes in her own life, she'd lost track of everything else. "Okay, okay…then we need to call Ryan."

Her cousin's tears increased as she made little sounds of distress. "No! He can't know! We haven't done anything. The baby isn't his!"

Oh no!

What was she to do? Tell Dia the truth? Let her continue to suffer in ignorance? There was no way she could allow her sweet cousin to agonize any longer. "The baby is his!"

Dia frowned and wiped at her eyes. "It isn't. I just told you, we haven't done anything. I meant sex. We haven't had sex!"

Celestia stared at her cousin, knowing she was in way over her head. "Dia, where are you and Ryan on things?"

She frowned. "What do you mean?"

"Do you love him?"

Dia nodded, tears still flowing like a river down her pale cheeks. "I do! I love him so much, but I can't tell him this! He won't understand! I don't understand! I have missed three periods! Maybe even four, I'm not sure at this point. I thought I was gaining a little weight, or I might have cancer or something your mother could fix quickly! But a baby? How do I explain that?"

Knowing she had no choice, Celestia patted Dia's hand. "You wait right here. I need to tidy up a bit, and then you're going home with me."

Dia nodded, the relieved look in her eyes telling Celestia she was happy to hand over anything related to a decision to another. Celestia hurried to the back and snatched her cell phone from her purse, hoping Ryan was where there was service. She knew they practically lived together at this point, and the reception on the mountain where Dia lived was ridiculously spotty, but she dialed anyway.

To her relief he picked up on the second ring.

"Do you know where Dia is?"

The panic in his voice caused hers to ease. "She's at the vet clinic with me. She's taken a pregnancy test. Time has run out, and I need you to get to my house quickly."

"I'm at her cabin. I'm afraid they might close the road, but I'm on my way."

Celestia chewed on her bottom lip then shook her head, even though he couldn't see it. "No. Meet me halfway. Go to my parents' cabin. The spare key is under the orange pot on the porch. I just found out they're out of town, and I need to check on the horses. Mom is still doctoring Cleo."

"Be careful! It's nasty out here."

Relieved they had a plan of action in place, Celestia threw the phone in her purse and headed back to the front where Dia sat staring into space. She smiled gently at her cousin, thankful all would be clear to her as soon as Ryan filled her in. "Let's go for a ride, cousin. I promise. Everything will be fine."

They hadn't gotten across town and even started the drive around Mystic Lake before Celestia doubted her words. Everything was hardly fine. Dia was still a hysterical mess, and visibility was extremely limited by the snow. She tried to follow her cousin's convoluted ramblings and offer sympathy whenever the opportunity arose, but just keeping her truck on the road proved a full-time occupation for both mind and body.

The exhaustion of all that had happened over the last month didn't help either.

She blew out a breath and tried to keep from letting the slow swishing of her wipers lull her into complacency. Or let the snowflakes coming at her, and then separating as they rounded the truck, send her into a hypnotic trance. In a way, it was good Dia was so vocal. It kept Celestia's heavy eyelids from closing, but it began to irritate too.

"Dia, please. This road is dangerous, and I'm weeks' worth of tired. Talk to me. But you have to calm down."

Immediate silence was welcome, but it made her feel like a heel. "I'm sorry. I know you're very upset. But I promise. Everything will be fine. Great in fact."

Celestia bit her bottom lip and dared to throw a look her cousin's way.

"Celestia!"

She jerked her head back and hit the brakes, skidded, fishtailed, and then stopped where a thick tree limb lay across the road. Shaking moved in and settled, making her force choppy breaths from her lungs. When she could finally take measured breaths, she turned to find Dia looking at her with wide eyes.

"Are you okay?"

Dia nodded. "Yes. You?"

Celestia nodded as well and blew out another breath. "That limb isn't too large. I'll drag it out of our way, so we can get going."

"I'll help."

Celestia reached across her cousin to stop her from opening the door. "No. You stay put. I'm already concerned…."

She didn't finish the sentence, but she didn't need to. Dia nodded slowly.

"Because I might be pregnant."

Celestia licked her lips, knowing she had to put a stop to the secret their families had harbored all these months. "Dia, there are things you need to know about your pregnancy and, well, other things."

Dia's blond brows pulled together, making parallel lines just above a nose that was identical to her own. Even though they were cousins, and each had two identical sisters, who weren't identical *at all* unless their genes were studied, she and Dia looked more alike than all the other female cousins. Their male cousins, Zeus, Apollo and Heracles, were perfectly identical in height and feature, as well as genetic makeup. The trio's only differences were bulk, or lack of it, and Heracles' need to have his brows shaped and his body waxed so the photographs that made him millions around the globe as an underwear model didn't remind women natural men came with body hair.

"Celestia?"

Realizing she'd zoned out for a moment, Celestia licked her lips, before biting the bottom one hard. Releasing it, she pressed both together, as her head and her heart took each other on in a battle of wills. Her head gave a good fight, but her heart won. She couldn't keep Dia in the dark any longer. "You lost your memories."

The neatly arched hairs again worked toward unibrowdom, while Dia's eyes held a hint of laughter.

"I did not."

"Dia, you did."

"I'd remember if I'd lost my memory."

Since it was such a normal Dia statement, Celestia let it go. "The moms wiped it clean at your request about four months ago."

Dia's mouth opened, then closed, and fear entered her light blue eyes. "Are you serious?"

Celestia exhaled, relieved she could finally look her cousin in the eyes, and not wince inwardly that they were all deceiving her. "Yes."

"Why would I ask them to do that? And why would they agree to it?" Horror filled her eyes. "Was I raped?"

Reaching out to lay a calming hand on Dia's arm, she shook her head. "No, you were madly in love, and you and Ryan were, well, *madly in love*."

Looking around the cab frantically before turning back to Celestia, Dia slumped in her seat. "That doesn't make any sense!"

"I know. And it would be better if Ryan explained it all because he knows details I don't. But the baby is his. And he loves you very much."

Tears spilled from Dia's eyes to fall from her long lower lashes. "I don't understand. Why wouldn't he have told me? Why hasn't anyone told me? Do you know how scared I've been? Do you know how scared I am? I don't know you people! And I don't want to see him!"

A sick feeling settled in Celestia's stomach, but she knew there was no other solution but for Dia to hear their story from Ryan himself. So this time her lie wasn't one of omission. It was blatantly premeditated.

"You don't have to see anyone right now, but I need to go to Mom's house to check on the horses they've been caring for, for me. No one expected this early season blizzard, and I doubt they prepared for it before they left."

Dia said nothing more, which suited Celestia just fine. She wanted so badly to fill her in on everything. At least she hadn't had to lie about that. She didn't know all the details, and those were the very things Ryan would have to provide if there was any chance of Dia being able to forgive any of them.

It didn't take as much effort to move the branch as she'd first feared, so Celestia was back in the warm cab of her truck within minutes. The drive up the mountain was another matter. She dared not go more than a few miles an hour. The last thing she wanted was to skid or fishtail with the solid wall of mountain on her side and the drop-off into Mystic Lake on Dia's. Thankfully, she could hand her cousin over to Ryan at her mom and dad's place. If she'd had to go all the way to Dia's cabin, they would be creeping up the mountain for well over the next hour.

"Just tell me one thing."

Celestia nodded but kept her eyes on the winding road.

"If this baby is Ryan's, I have to be what...four or five

months along?"

"Yes."

"Did it not occur to anyone I might need prenatal care?"

Celestia dared flash her cousin a smile. "My mom has been monitoring you regularly. Do you think she touches you as often as she does when we are all together because you've suddenly become her favorite?"

Dia shrugged, ignoring the teasing joke. "Your mom has always been a hugger."

Celestia nodded. "True. You know, before she got a handle on her gift to heal, she couldn't touch anyone without fixing whatever was wrong. Then when her powers went crazy, she burned anyone she touched. For years, she had to keep people at a distance, which I can't imagine. She's such a loving soul."

"Yeah, Mom told us about their lives before the curse was lifted. It must have been hell for them all."

Nodding, Celestia slid her a quick look. "All the moms have kept a close eye on you since you demanded your memory be wiped. And Uncle Tom had Mother Mountain add additional minerals in the water she supplies your cabin with, so you would get as much nourishment as you'd need."

"Hmmm."

Celestia frowned when the snowflakes grew bigger and danced down at them like little white spiked fairies. She enjoyed the show but worried it would only make her drive back down the mountain more scary, once she had delivered her charge and had indeed taken care of the horses she'd rescued from a neglectful owner.

"Can I ask you something else?"

Since Dia seemed so much calmer and asked in a way that helped Celestia to relax a little as she drove, she nodded. "Of course."

"Did I ever, you know, before I lost my memories of our time together... Um, well, did I ever talk about what it was like between Ryan and me?"

Celestia tried not to smile. "You mean like, did he kiss well?"

Dia giggled softly. "No. I know he kisses amazingly. We do that all the time! What I mean, is did I ever talk about what it was like to make love with him?"

Glad she couldn't peel her eyes from the tiny bit of road she could actually see, Celestia shook her head. "No. But it was easy to see you couldn't wait to be alone with him, whenever we were all together."

"I've wanted to make love with him so many times over the past months, but he never wanted to."

Celestia couldn't help but laugh. "Oh, I can guarantee he wanted to. All you have to do is be in the same room with you two and the hunger in his eyes for you says it all. But you chose a really decent guy for yourself, Dia. I'm sure he's been waiting for just the right moment, and I'd imagine he hasn't felt good about you not being told everything before now. His hands-off stance is quite gallant, actually. And the *not telling* part is by our three moms' orders. Not his."

"I'm so lost here."

Nodding, Celestia crept along. "I know. But everything will become clear shortly. I promise. Just trust that no one would ever do anything to hurt you."

"I know that. It's what has calmed me... A baby, Celestia! I'm going to have a baby! Ryan's baby!"

Even hearing fresh tears of joy in her cousin's voice, Celestia didn't have time to rejoice with her, because a bright beam of light shot straight out from the curve she approached. The indication a car headed their way caused every muscle in her body to clench in anticipation. She nearly hit the brakes as she considered stopping to wait until the car passed but was afraid if she didn't continue to creep forward, she might find herself unable to get started again on the slick, inclining road. "A car's coming."

"I see that. I hope it's going as slow as you."

"Me too. I'm afraid I'm going to meet it right at the sharpest point of the curve."

"Be careful!"

Celestia blew out a breath. "I will. I just hope they are too."

Trying not to let Dia's tension add to her own, she held tightly to the steering wheel and whispered a prayer. If the car coming at them was a local, she doubted meeting it would be much of an issue. She was pretty certain everyone who lived on the mountain, which basically consisted of her family and the native tribe of their Uncle Tom, had enough sense not to be out driving on an evening like this unless it was absolutely necessary.

If it weren't for Dia so desperately needing to hear the truth, and her own worry over the horses tugging at her heart, she sure as heck wouldn't be out.

As expected, the car met her in the curve, its bright lights hitting the edges of her vision and temporarily blinding her. But the other driver must have been as tense and cautious as she was. The car barely moved out of its own lane and into hers as they met. She heard both Dia's and her own sigh when they were once again the only ones on the dark and dangerous road.

"That was scary."

Celestia released a nervous laugh, and nodded. "Very. I hate Dead Man's Curve even in the best of conditions. At least we're almost to Mom and Dad's place. Thank God."

The next five minutes were less stressful, probably because there was an end to this trip in sight, if not physically, at least mentally. Celestia couldn't wait to get to her parents' house and could only hope Ryan had made it there safely, as well.

It was a relief to pull into the long driveway and see there were already tire tracks in the otherwise pristine snow. Though not nearly as long as the lane leading to Uncle Tom and Aunt Destiny's cabin, she still had to pass through a small forest before coming to the opening that led to the cabin she'd grown up in. The taillights from Ryan's truck and the plume of exhaust coming from it indicated he hadn't gone on into the cabin, and she had to press down a smile. He was such a decent guy. Even though he knew he'd be welcome to use the house for shelter, he had opted to wait for them to arrive.

She saw Ryan alight from the truck just as they pulled up next to him. Before she could turn off the engine, Dia was unbuckled and jumping from the truck, and Celestia's heart warmed as she watched her cousin fall into the arms of the man she loved.

Celestia laid her head back and gave herself a moment to relax every tense muscle. It was such a relief to be off the road and, even more so, to see her cousin's happiness was assured. Much too soon, Ryan, with Dia securely clasped to his side, opened her door. There were tears of joy in his eyes as well as her cousin's.

"You look beat."

Celestia laughed. "That isn't any way to talk to your future cousin-in-law."

His gorgeous grin met hers. "Come on out of there. We'll make sure you're okay, and then I'm taking Dia on up the mountain and home. We have a lot to talk about."

"Talking isn't all we're going to be doing," Dia put in with a giggle.

Large snowflakes fell on their heads, happiness shone from their eyes, and Celestia allowed only a seconds pang of envy. "You guys go ahead before it gets even worse than it is. I'll be fine here. The cabin will be warm soon enough if it isn't already, and the horses are surely in the new barn out back. Either way, I know this land like the back of my hand. I'll be fine."

Though he protested, Celestia firmly bid Dia and Ryan goodnight, relieved her cousin now knew she hadn't lost her mind. The day had been endlessly long, and all she wanted to do was shower, slide between the sheets of her childhood bed, and curl up with a good book until she couldn't keep her eyes open any longer. Unfortunately, that wasn't an immediate option.

Her day wasn't over. She let herself into her parents' home and immediately took off the snow-filled soft rubber-soled shoes she wore while in clinic. They were never meant to be worn in such weather and likely ruined, but there were more pressing things to worry over. Her white socks, equally soaked, were next, and she hurried across the living room to head back to the room she'd once shared with her sisters.

The bunk bed and twin that had filled the room was replaced with a queen-sized bed, covered in a handmade quilt, and a tall highboy that was both closet and dresser. The dark mahogany furniture was clearly the work of Dia's dad, Garrison White. Her sweetheart of an uncle was well known worldwide for his hand-tooled craftsmanship with custom-built furniture, as well as for the log homes he designed. As beautiful as it all was, she sighed, knowing there was likely nothing more than linens in the dresser, so she wandered to her parents' room.

Here the bed was a king, though the design was nearly identical to the one she soon planned to hibernate in. Another quilt, with a variety of protection symbols sewn within, covered the big bed, reminding her that her great-aunt Lune Brille Cavanaugh loved to create quilts now she'd gotten too old, *her words*, to continue to travel around the world all the time to keep the earth replenished.

Though from what her mother had told her, the great-aunt was busy playing Mother Nature, while she waited for one of her great-grandnieces or -nephews to pick up the torch.

That hadn't happened yet, but Dia was about to learn she wasn't only pregnant but had developed a gift she currently had no memories of. So maybe there was hope. It wouldn't be long before her mother and aunts, deemed *The Three*, millennia before their births, could restore Dia's memories, and she would once again know of her mystical abilities.

Relieved all was about to be right with their world, Celestia blew out a breath and searched through her mother's things until she found an outfit both blizzard-weather and poop-shoveling worthy. The thick sweater and low-riding jeans fit perfectly, since her mother still had both the style and figure of a young woman. Celestia went to the back door and lifted the thick jacket she knew her mother would have used for just such a chore, as well as rain boots only half a size too small.

Thankful she'd only have to be out in the barn for a short time, Celestia braced herself and opened the door. Before she could step out her cell phone sounded, and she looked to see a message from her sister, Soleli.

Mom and Dad not coming home for days. Serious stuff happening at Gavin's house. Will let you know as soon as I hear more.

Celestia quickly typed: *Okay. Thanks. At their place now. Tell them not to worry. The horses will be cared for. Would tell them myself, but busy right now.*

Will do. Be careful! Soleli responded.

Frowning when she realized the phone's battery meter was low, Celestia blanked her screen and dropped the phone in the pocket of the parka before snagging a handy flashlight and exiting the warmth of her parents' home to cross the snow-covered deck. Both before and after stepping down the stairs from the deck to the ground, her boots sunk a good four inches into the snow as she made a compacted trail with each step.

Though the parents' trip across the country had been unexpected, it didn't surprise Celestia at all her completely normal father and uncle Garrison had refused to be magically transported as sparkling dust, to get them there and back home quicker. She'd grown up knowing both men accepted the Cavanaugh women they'd wedded and the resulting children of their unions all had magical powers, but both stayed out of their wives' way when magic was implemented to solve one problem or another. To her knowledge, neither had ever allowed the magic to involve them directly. What *was* strange, however, was Uncle Tom and Aunt Destiny taking the longer route as well. Those two used their magic on a regular basis with no qualms, so something serious was up.

There was always something crazy going on in their individual lives. But until now, the entire family was always aware of every situation, *before* major moves were made to help whichever family member had issues. For the parents to leave without first informing the rest of them what was going down....

"This must be bad!"

Celestia shook her head when she realized she spoken aloud. "You're talking to the wind."

She laughed at herself as she gripped the flashlight tighter. "You're still doing it!"

Realizing she did so out of nervousness, Celestia clamped her lips shut as the hairs rose on her arms and unease settled across her shoulders. She scanned the area with the flashlight's strong beam. There was nothing to see but the thick flakes of snow and the obstructed yet darker image of the barn not too far ahead once she breached the line of trees separating what was considered her parents' acres of back yard. "I'm not nervous. This is home. I'm safe here."

Then stop talking to yourself!

Determined to do just that, she forged on, raising her legs just a little higher than normal as she stepped down on each stretch of freshly fallen snow. Before long, she was close to the pond her mother had forged with magic sometime before her birth. Celestia was certain it hadn't had time to freeze. She moved around the pond carefully, unable to prevent a smile as she thought of the last time the family had gathered at the parents' house, and her youngest sister, Luna, had been left with the charge of three panty-hat-wearing mermaids. Which took her thoughts further, and she wondered how her sister was doing in her new home at the submerged base of Mystic Mountain. How, if at all, would this weather affect her there?

Knowing she was scurrying to find things to occupy her mind, since being alone in this white wonderland was beginning to creep her out, Celestia breathed a sigh of relief when she entered through the barn's sliding door and was able to throw on the lights. The large structure held the smells of leather, horses, sawdust and hay. She even got an earthy whiff of the neatly stacked rectangular bales of alfalfa in the extended shed that ran the length of the stalled structure on the right. More comfortable now, and not only because she was out of the wind, Celestia started toward the far end of the barn. She needed to shut those large sliding wooden planked doors as well, to protect the horses from the elements and the possibility of getting lost in the forest beyond their field. Her biggest fear was they'd wander too far and the blizzard would continue to the point of disorientation. If it hadn't already.

The neighing of one of the horses was music to her ears, and she waited for the other's response while making her way to the two stalls her parents had fixed up to house their new friends. When there was no answering call, she moved faster, praying the animal was in the barn, too. Cleo, the large bay, stuck his head and front quarters out and bobbed the massive head up and down, his black mane rising and lowering off forehead and neck. She stepped up to him and held out her hand, and he immediately tilted his head so she could pet his jaw.

"I'll get your stall cleaned out, buddy. Tell me Cleopatra is in here too."

Cleo shook his head sharply and stomped with one hoof, making Celestia laugh. "You understood me?"

Not expecting a response, she was surprised when Cleo nodded then turned his head in the direction of the open doors. Celestia stared at him in confusion before deciding it coincidental that the horse had responded as he had. She shook off the notion he'd actually understood her and blew out an uneasy breath as she gently pushed against his shoulder. "Back up, boy. I'm locking you in, and then I have to go find Cleopatra."

Expecting compliance this time since she knew the animal was smart and well behaved, she was surprised when he shook his head sharply and moved forward. "Halt!"

Cleo shook his head again and stood firm.

Celestia didn't know what to do. Although there were still red lines and missing hair from horrible abuse, the big bay was now very healthy. It was hard to believe only two months before she'd found him neglected to the point of near starvation and no doubt whipped viciously, as well, since he had those long gashes across both flanks. Her parents had taken the horses in when she'd had animal control remove Cleo and Cleopatra from a farm down in the valley below, and they'd worked wonders in making the animals feel loved. She didn't want to do anything now to rekindle the fear that had once been in his large brown eyes, so she rubbed his strong jaw and spoke to him soothingly.

"It's cold and dangerous out there, Cleo. I need you stay here."

He shook his head again. This time she could have sworn she heard a whispered, "No," as well.

Celestia shook off the feeling she was stepping into over-exhaustion, and nodded. "Okay. You can go with me, but we go as a team, so you have to let me lead you."

Cleo shook his head again and walked past her to the stands holding richly oiled saddles. He nudged the larger of the two and then looked back at her.

Horses are really smart. This doesn't mean anything!

Celestia moved to stand before the saddle and glanced between it and Cleo. He stood patiently still, as if determined to wait her out. "Okay, big guy. I can't say I mind riding instead of walking."

His head danced up and down, and she couldn't help but laugh with the joy he brought to her. He was such a magnificent animal, and every time she had a chance to spend time with him, he won her heart even more. She saddled him and placed the bit into his mouth before sliding the halter upward and throwing the lead over his head. She didn't have to say anything more to him as she mounted and loosely took the reins. He turned and headed to the doorway leading to the back of her parents' property, and Celestia patted his neck. "Do you know where she is?"

Again, Cleo shook his head, but the back and forth motion was slower, as if he were actually considering his answer. This time Celestia didn't question his actions or even attempt to guide his movements. There was no doubt in her mind Cleo would find the filly even if they had to search all night. As tired as she was, she was more than willing to hand over the reins. She hunched over his back, and they left the barn. Immediately she was again pelted by the snow, and a shiver went up her back.

Chapter Three

Asking to be saved hadn't been the brightest of ideas. At least if the car had run him over, he wouldn't still be lying in snow dying a slow painful death. He'd already be dead.

An unexpected, strange whinnying-sound, forced him to pry open eyelashes that had frozen together. With his lashes still tangled, he squinted, trying to make out the approaching form through the snow falling into his blurred eyes. The long nose of a beautiful white face lowered to him and snorted, blowing what he was certain was horse snot and warm air, right into his face.

He reached up without thinking, and the animal blinked slowly, its long white lashes offset by what looked like black eyeliner outlining the enormous white and light blue eyes studying him. He ran his hand over the shiny black nose, wallowing in relief that another living being was present. He wasn't going to die completely alone. "Hi, beautiful."

A soft whinny was her response to his hoarse words, before she lifted her head, shook the snow off herself, and maneuvered her body so she nearly stood over-top of him. He felt a second of panic that she'd step on him, or lie on him. But she daintily shifted her feet instead, before her legs folded and she lowered her massive frame next to his nearly frozen one. She turned her head and looked back at him as steaming breaths and very real and welcomed heat radiated from her body, warming his. He closed his eyes, absorbing the heat, thankful he wasn't to die alone.

"Cleopatra!"

What? Who?

"Cleopatra! Where are you?"

He forced his eyes to open again knowing the voice he heard wasn't anything but the imaginings of his oxygen-depleted brain. Cleopatra...ah, yes. He was hallucinating. It was if he'd known her. That magnificent Ancient Egyptian....

"Cleopatra! Answer me! It's freezing out here!"

There it was again. That voice. Only this time it held fear. He tried to shake some sense into his head, but all he got was two ears full of snow. Which actually helped a little. Not much...just the discomfort registered, but that was something.

What if the voice I heard was real?

What if I'm not hallucinating?

It took effort to clear what seemed frozen cobwebs clouding his mind. He fought to keep his eyes opened since it was so much easier not to. He stared upward until he could make out the barely discernable gnarled bare branches and pine needle-covered limbs of the trees hovering over his head. Were it not for the massive amounts of snow covering the tops and sides of everything, he knew it would have been too dark to make out anything at all.

Because he had human eyes... *What? What?*

"Cleopatra!"

Confused by his thoughts, he could only stare up in fascination as a figure with an angelic face plopped herself down next to the horse lying at his side. At first he believed she'd come for him, but she chatted away to the horse as another one approached and looked at him with reproach in its large golden-brown eyes.

"Oh, Cleopatra! I'm so glad to have found you. Are you injured? Why didn't you come when I called? Cleo and I have been looking for you for hours!"

He watched as she patted the animal all over, seeming clueless that he was there too. A flash of irritation sparked from within, and whatever outward movement resulted drew her eyes his way.

"Oh! My! God!"

He couldn't correct her or even smile in relief that she'd noticed him, when the horse he now knew as Cleopatra struggled and rose up and onto her four hooves. The woman scrambled to him quickly, her hands all over him, knocking the snow from his form. She made all kinds of distress noises, as her mouth moved faster and faster. But he couldn't hear her words anymore as relief brought with it impending darkness. He gave into it this time, knowing his struggles to survive had come to an end.

****

Celestia's heart pounded painfully while she knocked the snow from the man's body. The shock of finding him was only compounded by the fact that he was completely naked and terribly injured, as was evidenced by the red stains once she removed the top layers of snow. She pulled her cell phone from her jacket and frantically spun the screens until she found the one that turned her phone into a flashlight, since the batteries on the one she'd used for the past hours had died out a short while ago.

Her breath caught when she opened his eyelids, and his pupils reacted slowly to flashing the beam left and right across his face. At least they reacted, which meant he wasn't yet dead. She turned back to find Cleo and Cleopatra only a couple of feet away. Both watched her as they stood side by side, the steam from their collective breaths hanging in the still air. Hoping they could help in some way, she rose and walked back to the male. "Hey, buddy. We need to get that man to the cabin. Can you help me?"

Cleo nodded, and this time she didn't even question it. He moved in closer, with her following, and stopped to lower his head and shake. The reins slid over his head and fell onto the snow at the man's side.

"Good thinking. We have to pull him out first." Celestia looked around and spied several fallen limbs. She chose one that still had a large spread of branches and dragged it closer to her patient, wishing she had either the necessary mystical powers to make all this easier on them both or a travois to transport him back to the cabin.

Although her male cousins, her female cousins and her sister Luna all received their magical gifts, Celestia was losing the battle of worry she and her next youngest sister, Soleli, were destined to be normal. If one could deem wielding no magic was what made a person so. Were it not for the silver elements of blood in their veins there was no physical evidence she and Soleli were a part of the mystical line of Cavanaugh women who came before. All they were was odd. The silver blood not only didn't do anything helpful, it would only create problems were anyone outside of the family to know of it.

Not having time to worry over that right now, or anything else save her exhaustion, Celestia retrieved the coiled rope and wool blanket she'd left hanging from Cleo's saddle with the expectation of using both on Cleopatra should the need have arisen. Now, she just hoped the mare would follow them back on her own.

But what would she do with this man once she was back at the house? Over the hours she'd been searching for the horse, the snow had deepened. Like crazy deepened. They'd had several serious snow events on the mountain during her lifetime. They'd made winter fun for her as a child. But she couldn't remember a time it had snowed so much, so quickly. It was entirely possible her mother's presence had held the local weather in check. That was her gift. And now Haven Cavanaugh-Hansen was across the country....

Celestia shook off the fear. Those whose powers protected them all were not present. She was an adult. A smart woman. And would handle this situation as such. It didn't matter why the weather was so crazy. Nothing mattered at the moment but getting him out of the elements. She couldn't even worry over the possibility of an injured spine or broken bones. If he froze to death, those wouldn't make a difference anyway.

Still, hoping she did less harm than good, Celestia dug him out and rolled him onto the spread of smaller branches, resting his head in the thick dried leaves toward the broken end. It took even more time to tie the rope just above his head, and to the saddle's horn, but after what felt like too much time had passed she was satisfied it was as secure as she could make it.

Thankful the snowfall had eased a little, Celestia threw the blanket over him and tucked it in at his sides. Weary, her back hurting, she stood up straight and looked down, praying his body was well enough protected, on both the top and at his back. "You stay put. I'm too tired to do all this again."

It took more effort than she thought herself capable of, but she finally pulled herself back into the saddle. Although the stud fidgeted nervously, Cleo remained standing in the same spot through the entire process, a testament to his gentle and obedient nature. He only took a step forward once she clicked her heels at his flank. "Go as slow as is safe, boy. But get us back to the barn quick as you can."

Fortunately, she didn't have to say anything to Cleopatra. The white filly walked slowly at the side of branch carrying the injured man as if she checked on his every breath. Celestia thanked her silently and turned back to watch ahead as Cleo carried them toward the barn. Since he took a direct path, which hadn't been the case when they'd been out looking for the mare, the trip back was considerably shorter than the trip out. But because they had to go so slowly, to not throw their charge off the branch, dawn was breaking by the time the snow-capped barn came into view.

And it started snowing heavily again.

"I'm too tired for this!"

Cleo swung his head around to look back at her, and Celestia leaned forward and patted his neck. "I know, you've been a real trouper, too. Let's get this guy to the house, and then I'll come back and take care of you and Cleopatra later. Okay?"

Once inside the barn she dismounted and immediately went back to check on the man, afraid she'd find him already dead. It was a relief to feel a pulse at his wrist, as well as see his chest rise and lower beneath the blanket that was still firmly in place. Knowing she'd need help to get him into the house, Celestia pulled her phone from her jacket, but it had run on the same charge for two days now, and the single flash of red at the top made her heart sink. "Oh dear."

As soon as she hit the screen to wake it up, a message flashed across the front before the screen went black. "Perfect."

With the slim hope her parents had a charger in the house that would work for her phone as well, Celestia made short work of securing Cleopatra in a stall and closing the big doors they'd just entered through. She glanced in and breathed a sigh. Both animals had enough supplies to keep them fed and watered until she could get the man settled and, hopefully, even take a little nap.

A moan came from behind Cleo, and she hurried around the large animal to find the man struggling to shrug off the blanket. "Oh, no, no, no!" She knelt down and pulled the cover back over his shoulders. "Don't move."

His eyes fluttered, opened, closed, and opened again, and Celestia nearly choked on the relieved breath that filled her lungs. "Please. Don't move yet. I don't know how badly you're injured."

He nodded slowly before turning his head to look around.

"You're in a barn. Cleopatra found you, and she's taken care of you. But now I need to get you to the house. Can you be still until I can get you there?"

He nodded again and closed his eyes.

Celestia didn't waste any time. She walked Cleo to the far end of the barn and opened one of the big doors. If she could get them to the house quickly, and if the man could help her help him inside, it solved at least one of her problems.

Cleo allowed her to mount, and he headed straight toward the structure that was a beacon as far as she was concerned. It took less than half the time it would have taken were she not on the large animal's back, but the closer they got the more anxious she was to arrive, and it seemed like forever. When Cleo stopped and turned so the large branch lay parallel with the deck, Celestia dismounted and walked around to kiss the horse on his jaw. "You are a prince! Thank you, my friend. As soon as I untie the rope, please go back to the barn and stay there." His large head nodded up and down. Celestia shook her own head, amazed they were so in sync.

Because her fingers had moved past stiff to sore, it took some effort to pry the rope loose, but once she did, Cleo moved away, following her instructions. She turned back to find the man staring up at her, and thoughts of her four-legged friend fled. She knelt. "Can you help me get you up?"

"Name?"

Since the one word seemed to take so much effort,

she'd rather he not try to talk. But she had so many questions herself, she answered. "Celestia. Yours?"

"Sab..." he shook his head. "Sabbububuh."

Celestia placed her fingers lightly across his stammering lips, worried the panic in his eyes would make the next few moments even harder than they already promised to be. "It's okay. You can tell me later. You're freezing. I need to get you inside and thaw you out. And me too."

He nodded and struggled to sit up. "No! Don't move yet. I need to check you out a little first. I should have already done this, but I needed to get us back here as quickly as I could."

He settled with a groan, and Celestia took it as compliance. She steeled herself to examine his body as she pulled off her gloves and placed a hand on his forehead. It was hot, and she feared the redness of his cheeks wasn't just an indication his skin was chapped. She examined his head injury then moved on down to the bruising of his shoulder. It looked as if one side of him was much worse off than the other, but she was just getting started. She pulled the blanket back over that area and uncovered his chest. She winced when he moaned and jerked when she touched the ribs of his injured side but forged on until she came to the line of dark hair below his belly button.

Taking a deep breath, she uncovered his hips, and only allowed her eyes to skim his genitals long enough to determine his penis seemed unharmed, as it lay dormant against one thigh. She quickly sent her attention to the blackening and bloody hip, knowing she'd have to get an antibiotic in those gashes as soon as possible. But first, she had to press her fingers into his wounds to make sure the hip hadn't dislocated.

"Cold!" he shouted, as his body went into shivers.

Celestia flashed him a nod. "I know. I'm almost done.

I think you have broken ribs. But I need to check your legs to see if you can use them. I need to get you into the house, and I really need you to help me if you can."

He nodded once, sharply, before she pressed and maneuvered first one leg and then the other. It was clear the bones were intact, but the injured side of him continued to show what a chore it would be for him to assist her once they got him up.

"This is going to hurt like hell."

It took only a few minutes of his sweat-on-the-brow floundering for Celestia to realize she'd have to do most of the work. By the time she pulled him off the many small branches and dried leaves that had carried him to the house, and he was on his knees inches from the snow-covered steps to the deck, they were both huffing and puffing.

"I'm going to slide up under your arm on the least injured side and carry as much of your weight as I can. But I need you to help me."

Looking completely exhausted, he nodded, and Celestia moved as quickly to position herself to lift his weight. "Try to grab the railing, and try to stand up."

It was obvious just lifting his massively muscular arm took nearly more strength than he had, but Celestia was relieved to see he did everything he could to assist her. She pulled his icy body next to hers, not the least bit concerned for his nakedness now. It was the first time she'd seen a nude male since her boy cousins were younger, with no qualms about swimming naked and acting like the fools they were.

Of course, she'd grown up in a family where nudity was considered as natural as breathing, so she hadn't thought a thing about it until the day of the Ascension Ceremony when she and her identical sisters, her three female cousins and three male cousins, all turned fifteen.

After that, nothing was ever the same again. For any of them.

A grunt from the man at her side, as he struggled to stand upright, pulled her from her familial musings. She didn't have time to think about her mystical family or all their oddities. Right now, she had a very human male in need of medical treatment she wasn't sure she was qualified to handle. But first, she had to get his massive form inside.

The few steps up and onto the deck weren't as hard as she'd expected them to be. The open area between the landing and the back door to her parents' cabin was another matter. Her very heavy charge had nothing but her to brace himself with, and she was certain, though she was tall for a woman and amateurishly athletic, he was going to break her back. Or at least the shoulder on which he supported himself.

Reaching the door brought a fog-filled airy sigh of relief from them both, and Celestia was thankful he had enough presence of mind to support himself against the log structure that was her parents' home while she opened the doors to allow them to enter the kitchen.

He didn't reach for her as she'd expected but used the doorframe, followed by the counter topping the kitchen cabinets right inside the door, and then lunged from one piece of furniture to the next, until he was able to fall onto the living room couch. Celestia hurried behind him, cringing at all the water they were leaving on her parents' wood flooring.

"I'd rather get you to a bed. Or in a warm shower." She threw two of her mother's handy decorative throws over him, then ran back to get them both a glass of the ice cold water from the tap, hoping the magic in the water piped in from the top of Mystic Mountain would rejuvenate her and hydrate him.

He refused it at first, and she understood he was too

exhausted to want to lift his head. She gently forced him by supporting his head and holding the glass to his lips until he gave in. Once he started drinking, he placed a shaking hand over hers, and tilted the glass a little more so he could consume it all as he stared into her eyes.

She moved the glass away, and looked him over. "Tell me where you hurt most."

He lay back and licked lips so chapped they were cracked and held dried blood. Celestia gave him a moment, relieved to see his eyes, as deeply blue as her cousin Sapphire's, were clearer than they had been since she'd found him.

"Cold."

"Stay put. I'll be right back. I don't think you're going to thaw out without a lot of help." She didn't add that she couldn't believe he hadn't already frozen to death or that she had no idea how or when he'd landed in the woods of her parents' property... or why he had done so naked. Questions raced through her mind, but she held them back as she ran to the room she'd planned to sleep in, pausing only long enough to raise the thermostat. It took only minutes to strip the bed of the light quilt and pull an electric blanket from the linen closet to cover the sheets again. She plugged the cord in, turned the dial to high, threw the quilt back on top, and hurriedly retraced her steps to find him pulling himself into a nearly sitting position. Surely falling to the floor—his certain next destination—spelled disaster for his already abused body. "Whoa!"

He looked up at her, his eyes filled with desperation. Celestia moved to him quickly. "I'll help you to the bed."

He shook his head and pointed to his blanket-covered crotch. Celestia cleared her throat. "Bathroom?"

He nodded, and she had to hurry to capture his arm when he rose suddenly then swayed. "Need to go bad, huh?"

He nodded again and allowed the blanket to fall to the floor. Celestia saw no point in making an issue of it. It was obvious the man had other things on his mind. But she couldn't help but comment as they crossed the living room, "You need to stay wrapped up as much as possible. I just kicked up the thermostat, but it isn't all that warm in here yet, and your body needs to heat up."

He groaned a sound she took for agreement, but she wasn't sure he paid any attention to her. "Okay. You're in a hurry."

He allowed Celestia to lead him to the bathroom she and her sisters had once shared with their parents. "Are you okay by yourself?"

At his sharp nod, she backed out, and closed the door. "I'm going to build us a fire in the living room. It will warm up the cabin more quickly. Will you be okay?"

She waited and heard the hard hit of what she knew was a male peeing into the toilet, followed by what sounded like a bark of pain. Celestia bit her lip, not certain if she should step back inside or wait for his response.

"Go! Please."

Relief he didn't need her inside with him washed through her, or perhaps what she felt was dizziness from exhaustion. She wasn't sure which but knew she didn't have time to ponder either. She hurried to the living room's large stone fireplace, thankful the kindling and logs had already been stacked upon the grate in preparation for whenever winter weather would hit.

It often did with little warning on the mountain. Even sometimes, like now, in autumn.

Thinking she would kiss her parents on the lips right now if she could, she ignited the kindling with one of the long matches kept in a decorative box sitting near the end of the wide hearth. Less than a minute later crackling, popping and the tiny sparks shooting in all directions were accompanied by smoke rolling out toward her face, reminding her she needed to open the flue. Immediately the smoke sucked up the chimney, and the height of the flames increased upward instead of rolling smoke around the logs.

Celestia closed her eyes and allowed the heat to radiate warmth toward her, only then realizing how chilled she felt from the inside out. Wishing she could stay put, she struggled to her feet. Her own body had just about reached its limit. She'd been awake and working for over twenty-four hours. As soon as she could get her mystery man settled, she had to lie down too.

Or fall on her face.

She stopped at the closed door and heard nothing coming from inside. "Are you okay in there?"

"Yes."

"Do you need my help?"

"Yes."

Celestia steadied herself. Everything had happened so fast she hadn't had time to analyze any of it. She was in her parents' cabin with a complete stranger. A naked male who could be an ax murderer for all she knew. She blew out a breath and opened the door to find him bracing himself with his palms against the wall behind the commode. It was the first time she had a chance to *really* look him over, without distraction.

The man was several inches taller than her, with a scratched and bruised body that was as purely toned as any she had ever seen. She pulled her gaze upward quickly when it reached his bloody toes, taking in his past-the-shoulder length long dark hair, still glistening with melted snow. The tangled mess had pine needles and tiny pieces of bark sticking out here and there, and it took restraint to keep from moving forward to pull the objects out. Since his head hung downward, she could only see hints of the features beneath, but the strain he'd endured was reflected in the tightness of his jawline.

"Would you like me to help you shower?" Celestia winced, wondering why that was the first thing to pass her lips, but she really had no idea how to proceed from here.

He turned his head and she caught a glimpse of his face, but much of it was still covered with matted black waves.

"Please. I'm dirty."

She nodded and stripped off the parka and kicked off the boots as she passed inches behind his perfectly rounded, horribly scratched, naked butt. She made her way to the large glass-enclosed tiled shower, standard for all the cabins her family members owned. With the design and construction talents of her uncles Garrison and Tom, and her cousin by marriage, Nicolae, there wasn't a mundane bathroom to be found for any members of the Cavanaugh clan residing on Mystic Mountain. Every structure, every piece of hardware, and every shower stall including this one, would easily compare to those in multi-million dollar homes throughout the country. But with the exception of Uncle Tom and Aunt Destiny's cabin, the homes were mostly humble and rustic in overall design.

She opened the glass door and stepped into what amounted to its own small room, stopping only to decide how many of the showerheads to turn on. Deciding he was probably too bruised and battered to want the water hitting him from all sides, she chose to only use the large one coming down from the tiled ceiling. It would feel more like heavy rainfall, rather than several harder shooting sprays.

Which meant, she too, would get soaked.

Celestia pushed the appropriate buttons and stepped back quickly, thinking her family's shower fetish a little over the top. But who was she to judge? She'd gotten to grow up playing within them and had always loved the extravagance herself. She looked down at her soaked clothing and decided it didn't matter. The last thing she was going to do was get naked with the stranger waiting for her help.

Since the floor was the same tile as the shower, Celestia didn't hesitate to step out. "It's ready."

He pushed away from the wall, and she had to hurry to capture him around his wide ribcage and arms to keep him from falling backward onto his butt. He cried out. Trying to ignore his pain so she could do what must be done, Celestia focused on his rock solid form and weight that seemed even heavier than she remembered. Perhaps because she was already so tired, it took everything she had not to go down with him.

"Help me," she grunted, determined to stay on her own feet. Thankfully, he made the effort to take his weight from her and was able to stand up straight. "Good grief, what do you weigh?"

He glanced down at her as she looked up, and her breath caught. His face was strong, angular, his sapphire blue eyes intense as they stared back into hers. His features were a work of art, the slight shadow of an emerging beard only adding to the masculinity of his otherwise unblemished face. She felt captured by his eyes, almost drowning in their hold.

Celestia shook her head and looked down and wished she hadn't. There, standing proudly if not a little bluish, was the well-endowed penis of an aroused male. She closed her eyes. Not because she was frightened, or even appalled, but because something inside of her lit as if a switch flicked on, and she had no idea what to do with the shaking coming from inside.

"I don't know."

She looked back up into his face. "What?"

"I don't know what I weigh."

"Oh...."

His wide lips chose that moment to lift and part,

showing a set of pearly white teeth that had to have known braces. That odd thought was followed by another. The desire to take his lips with her own was almost too overpowering to resist.

She did. But just barely. And sanity returned. "Help me get you into the shower."

He said nothing as his gaze traced the outline of her face, finally to land on her lips. She licked them and then realized she had. Heat filled what only moments before was a still chilled face. "The shower," she said, meaning for it to sound like a command, not an invitation. His eyes widened, and sparkled, indicating he'd noticed the difference.

"You are very beautiful."

Celestia didn't smile in response, nor could she return the very true sentiment. He was a stranger. Naked. And aroused. But even more shocking, she was too. Other than naked.

Swallowing, she broke eye contact again and loosened her hold, relieved he seemed capable now of standing on his own. "Go ahead and bathe. Shampoos and soaps are on the built-in shelves inside. Take as long as you need. And I'll get you something to wear."

She couldn't wait for his response or even stay long enough to see he made it into the shower stall on his own. She had to get away from him. And she needed to pull herself together.

Celestia shut the bathroom door behind her, though she had no idea why. Perhaps to distance herself from his gorgeous body? Or to remind herself that she should? Her mind was in turmoil, and buzzing...surely just from the lack of sleep.

"I'm punch-drunk from exhaustion."

Telling herself that was all that was going on with her, Celestia stripped off her wet clothing and headed to the kitchen to drop them into the sink before scurrying to her old room. Although she would have loved a shower as well, the cabin had only one. Even with her family having more than three thousand years of acquired wealth on her mystical mother's side, on top of her father's heart surgeon's income, another one hadn't ever happened. Her mother was of the earth and believed there was no reason in having more than one needed or using the resources of the planet beyond what little people really required.

After entering her old room, it took only moments to remember her mistake, so she hurried back up the hallway to the living room and climbed up to her parents' loft.

Thankful her mother still had such a great figure, Celestia chose a winter pajama set that was a T-shirt and thick plush bottoms. She pulled them on, and searched for something similar in her father's drawers. Of course, the bottoms were less plush and probably not long enough given her visitor's height, but at least they would cover his body.

Oh, man... his body!

Celestia shook off the image that instantly filled her mind. She didn't want to think about that. She had to see to his needs. Find out who he was, and whom she should contact to get him back where he belonged. There was no doubt he belonged to someone... A girlfriend? A wife? Was he someone's father? No doubt, he was someone's son....

Get a grip!

Oh, man, she so needed to get a grip!

Celestia allowed herself a moment before heading back down the stairs. What was it about him that had pulled such a strong and strange reaction from her? She wasn't one to react to a man's looks or build or anything, really. She'd spent years, year-round, working toward her veterinary degree. And, though she'd been extremely focused, she'd come into contact with several good-looking men over the years. She'd dated some real eye-candy, but none had held her interest enough for it to go beyond dinner and sometimes a movie. She'd watched her cousins and her youngest sister find the men that completed the lives they wanted, but she hadn't ever thought much more about the gorgeous men they dated or married, other than they were a good fit into their weird, mystically gifted family.

But not once, ever, had she had a physical reaction to anyone.

A small sound from below alerted her to the possibility the man was done, though she couldn't really identify what the sound was. It wasn't loud enough to indicate he'd fallen and hit something. She climbed down, only to find him leaning against the log wall where the hallway ended at the living room's entrance.

And to her relief, he had the towel wrapped around his hips.

Celestia hurried down to him holding out the clothing she'd borrowed from her dad. "The shirt might be a little tight at the shoulders, and the sweats a little short, but it will help to warm you. Of course, we need to address your injuries before you cover them up."

He nodded to her and glanced at the now roaring fire. "That helps. It's as strange to feel heat as it was to feel so cold. I definitely like heat better."

Celestia nodded, though she had no idea why. He seemed none the worse for wear mentally, considering all he'd been through. That meant it was time to get answers. "Now that you're clean, let's get you fixed up." He finally took the clothing from her outstretched hand and reached for the corner of the towel. Celestia turned her back to him quickly and held out her hand. "Give me the towel. I'll take care of it."

The weight of it landing on her hand reminded her a naked male was standing at her back. She walked to the kitchen sink and gathered her wet clothing but stopped there, not willing to turn back just yet. She heard his movements, his grunts, and something that could have been a curse. She knew she should be there helping him, but she just couldn't move.

"I have the pants on."

Celestia glanced his way reluctantly and then exhaled. "That's good. Now go back to the couch and wrap up with the throws while I take these to the washer."

His brows drew together. "You are uncomfortable with me."

Celestia nodded. "Yes. But only because I don't know you."

"Because you have seen me naked." He countered.

She cleared her throat. "That too."

His lips lifted and his brows settled back into place. "It is a very American reaction."

She turned to him fully, still not willing to move toward the hallway, which led back to the laundry room, until he moved away. "Are you not American, then?"

His brows were close again, and he seemed to hesitate answering. Celestia waited, hoping to learn what she needed to know quickly. If there was somewhere he needed to be, someone who needed to know about his…situation, she needed to know it immediately. Looking into his amazing eyes, at the beauty of his still half-naked form, was making her more uncomfortable by the minute.

Chapter Four

"What's your name?"

It felt as if his chest froze and air couldn't get into his lungs. She'd asked him that question before, and he'd struggled to remember. Sabastian Envoi was what flowed through his mind, but it didn't feel right allowing it to pass his lips. He scrubbed at his face with his palm to buy time, but the sensation of numbing pain from the light friction distracted him. He looked at his palms wondering why he'd even noticed.

"Are you ill?"

He lifted his gaze to the woman...*Celestia*. He was taken aback by her beauty; he had been each time he'd focused on her face. Her hair was the purest of whites, like the snow-covered mountain from which she'd saved him. Her eyes were large, the color combination one he'd never seen before. The irises held shimmering flecks of gold that almost seemed to change at times to brown but were predominantly such a dark green that when shadowed by her long thick lashes, they seemed almost black. Those dark lashes surrounding her eyes were a stark contrast to the fairness of her skin and hair. Were it not for her eyes and the plumpness of lips he could only identify as a frosted-mauve, he imagined she would almost fade into invisibility against a white wall.

"Sir? Are you ill?"

He shook his head. "No. I'm sorry. I'm a little confused right now."

Her lips relaxed into a smile. "That makes complete sense. You've been through a lot, I imagine. Most of your contusions don't look too bad, but it wouldn't hurt to check you out more thoroughly. I'm not a doctor, but I am a vet, so I can treat your minor injuries. Do you feel you have any that would need a doctor's attention?"

He took a moment to move enough to determine he was very sore, especially on the side where he'd landed on the road. But everything worked without any sharp pains. "I think I'm okay."

Her nod was clearly one of relief.

"You need to lie down and rest for a while then. I've prepared a bed for you, and it will be toasty by now. Between an electric blanket and the fireplace heat, you should warm quickly." She bit her bottom lip and then moved closer. "I'll get supplies and put antibiotic ointment on the cuts. Why don't you head back to the room across from the bathroom, and lie down?"

He nodded, but stayed where he was. "I think my name is Sabastian."

She almost smiled, then didn't. "You think?"

He nodded. "Yes. When you asked my name earlier, the name Sabastian Envoi came to me, but it didn't feel right."

Celestia moved closer and looked his face over. The fresh, outdoorsy scent of her filled his nostrils with pleasure, as did the look of concern in her eyes.

"You have a bad bruise on this side of your face. I noticed it all down that one side. Maybe I shouldn't let you rest. You could have a concussion." She swayed and then jerked to stand up straight.

He looked her over and felt horrible. "You are tired."

Her lips opened into a wide smile as laughter passed them. "I'm exhausted. But that isn't important at the moment."

"It is. You're about to fall over."

Her brows drew together. "Really, I'm fine. Nothing a

gallon or two of something caffeinated wouldn't fix."

He took a deep breath and let it out slowly. "I appreciate your concern, but I'm okay. I'll go lie in the bed if that is what you wish, but you need to lie down too. I promise. I won't touch anything."

He could tell by the subtle way her face altered, she took his meaning wrong. "I meant in the house, but that includes you too. I only wanted to assure you that you have nothing to worry about from me. You need rest more than I do."

She stared at him a moment before speaking. "I really do need to sleep. But you shouldn't. I can get you a book to read while I lie down for a little while, but only if you promise to wake me if you feel like you are sleepy or dizzy?"

He nodded. It was obvious she wasn't going to take care of herself if he did otherwise. "I promise. And a book sounds good."

"What do you like to read?"

He frowned and looked at his hands, wondering why the thought of holding a book and reading it felt like something he'd never done before. Of course, he would have had to. Wouldn't he? No one could be his age....

"Sabastian?"

He dragged his gaze upward to find her still studying him. "Yes?"

"Do you remember anything about yourself?"

It nearly choked him to answer her. "No. I don't. Um...not really."

She nodded. "It's okay. You've obviously been through physical trauma, and you don't know what else. If the roads weren't so perilous, I'd take you to town and to the hospital to get you checked out. But you're moving pretty well. I don't think your ribs are broken, and your eyes are clear, so I don't think we are dealing with anything too serious. Just promise me, once we attend to your cuts, you'll stay awake. At least until I wake up from a little nap."

"I will."

She nodded. "Thank you."

Her words were so heartfelt, Sabastian knew she really was about to collapse. "My cuts are fine. You go lie down."

"No." She exhaled heavily. "I need to take care of you first, or I won't be able to sleep."

"You are an angel of mercy," he said and then felt dizzy. Determined not to let her see he might indeed have a concussion, he smiled. "You said you have a book?"

She motioned for him to follow her, and he did, right into the room she'd indicated he was to go. "Hop in bed. I'll get medical supplies and a book and be right back."

Sabastian waited until she left and slowly climbed onto the bed, trying not to moan aloud as he settled into a comfortable position. His body was one big mass of aches, especially on the side she'd indicated was mostly all bruises. He looked himself over, realizing the muscles beneath the discolored skin would pain him for days. But as she'd said, he could move all his parts with barely more pain that was already there.

What was more troubling than his physical condition was his loss of memory. He knew what all the items in the room around him were, but beyond finding himself in the snow-covered woods only hours before, he couldn't remember anything about his life.

"I hope you like this. My aunt writes paranormal novels. I haven't had a chance to read them since I've been consumed with getting my degree, then taking over the vet practice in town, but I'm told they're very good, even a little scary. Hopefully it will keep you awake."

Sabastian took the book from her hand and glanced at the cover. It was a deep purple, with roiling pink and varying shades of purple clouds. Multiple flashes of lightning shot from those clouds, looking like they would actually electrocute anyone holding the book.

The title wasn't as large as the author's name, both a stark white that jumped from the pages. There were also three much smaller lines about three identical sisters, who had three individual mystical gifts, and lived under a three-thousand-year-old curse, which he supposed was to pique interest when the book was sitting on the shelf. His definitely piqued, he set the book aside and prepared to be touched by those long-fingered, beautiful hands.

Celestia maneuvered herself so she sat at his side, and placed a small red box in front of her. He watched silently as she flipped up the top, and a small white cross flashed across his vision before the lid fell back upon the sheet. Something about the cross bothered him, but for the life of him, he couldn't figure out why.

"Let's start with the cut on your head and the scratches on the side of your face. They don't look too bad, but I imagine they sting. My father is a doctor. I sure wish he was here to make sure you don't need stitches."

Sabastian automatically placed his fingers on the side of his head. "I didn't even notice pain there until now."

Celestia grinned, as she pulled latex gloves from the medical kit. "Then shame on me for pointing it out."

She was so beautiful it took his breath. He blinked and looked down, not wanting his reaction to such physical perfection to be reflected in his eyes and noticed by her. He knew she was a little nervous to be stuck in a secluded cabin with him. He didn't want to do anything to cause her further concern.

"I'm sure I would have noticed if I didn't already hurt so much everywhere else." He glanced up to see her look of compassion as her gloved fingers touched his and pulled his hands away from the cut on his scalp. Fortunately, there was only a little blood on his fingertips.

"I'll put this on them, and then we'll check out everything else."

Celestia opened a small jar and dipped out a tiny bit of salve before running it gently over his forehead, cheek, and jaw. He watched as she took a deep breath before placing a portion on his head after separating a section of hair. She kept her gaze locked on her mission, and Sabastian felt his neck heat when her gaze lowered to collide with his. Awareness passed between them, and he felt his body stir. He clasped her wrist and gently pulled her hand away.

"I can take care of it now. You need to lie down and rest yourself. I promise, my head is clear, I'm not dizzy or nauseated, and I won't go to sleep."

She swallowed, and nodded slowly. "I think that's a good idea."

Sabastian held in the smile that threatened to reshape his lips. The more he moved them, the more they hurt. "Me too."

Celestia removed the gloves and then arose. "I'll be in my parents' bed, up in the loft. If you need me for anything, please, don't hesitate to call."

He nodded and watched as she left the room. He blew out a long breath, only then realizing how full his lungs had been. For a moment, Sabastian did nothing but stare at the empty doorway and then made himself look away. His body was in major pain, but now, not all of it had to do with his fall.

Fall?

Not knowing where that thought came from he focused on his body. The tent under the sweat pants Celestia had loaned him was obvious and strangely satisfying. He was certain it was also what had made her so eager to let him care for himself. He ignored it and used the salve to soothe the scrapes from his shoulder to hips, then slid more down between the sweatpants on the leg that pained him most. Within minutes, there was a cooling sensation, followed by an easing of discomfort. It wasn't until he replaced the small glass lid that he noticed there was nothing on the pot's exterior to identify what the healing balm was or what it was meant to do.

It didn't matter. He already felt a little better.

Sabastian replaced the jar inside of the red box and sat it on the small table at the bed's side before lifting the book he was determined would keep him alert until Celestia awoke. He ran his fingers over the cover, liking the sensation of the paper against his fingertips. The title, *Mystical Thunder*, and author's name, Rayne Cavanaugh-White, pressed outward slightly, giving his fingertips the sensation of flowing over shallow mountains. The cover art of rolling clouds, which had looked static at his last viewing, suddenly seemed to swirl before his eyes.

He blinked and looked again, relieved the clouds were now still. Swallowing, he lifted a hand to his scraped temple and rubbed gently. Though still slightly sore, it was definitely better than it had been before Celestia applied the salve. Nevertheless, he was almost certain now the hit to his head had caused more damage than met the eye.

Sabastian opened the book and skimmed over the dedication. He turned another page, ready to settle in and start reading, but a drawing of a dragon stopped him cold. He rubbed at the sharp pain settling between his eyes as he studied the unusually shaped head and even stranger shaped eyes. The dragon's look of desperation felt familiar. Something flashed, like a snapshot of memory, but was gone before he grasped it. A chill washed over him, and Sabastian turned another page, telling himself he hadn't done it any quicker than he would have at any other time... If only he could remember doing it before.

The story started with a bang.

Filled with colorful and provocative words that

captured his imagination immediately, the plot was both chilling and enticing at the same time. He repositioned himself to ease the ache that had settled in his lower back. He read on quickly, anticipating each upcoming paragraph, then grinning when something happened completely different than he'd expected. He grimaced at the deviant behavior of the man he was certain was the villain, while light coming through the window across the room shifted. It lightened and darkened the room by turns. He barked out a laugh many times when a surprising twist of action amused or shocked. He tensed when he feared what came next. It wasn't until his stomach grumbled that he realized the morning had turned into late afternoon, and he lifted his head from the addictive prose to listen, only to experience complete silence.

Noticing the chill for the first time, he placed the book on the table at his side and rose from the bed gingerly. Thankfully, he ached only a little, but the stiffness in his hips and legs made moving difficult. Stretching helped to loosen him up some, and he crossed to the doorway and then the hallway, to the nicely appointed bathroom he hadn't really paid any attention to before.

There was a second of hesitation as he anticipated using the toilet. The first time he had it hurt, almost as if his penis hadn't known what to expect. But he'd been near-frozen at the time. Fortunately, this time, there was nothing more than relief. He squeezed and shook himself out and flushed the toilet, then moved to the nice copper bowl-topped vanity to wash his hands. The scent of the liquid soap was woodsy with a hint of pine. It made him think of the freshness of a pristine forest, the shampoo he'd used, and the woman he hoped was getting the rest she so sorely needed. The androgynous fragrance was pleasant, and it would complement either man or woman equally. He had no idea why he was giving it so much thought.

Sabastian looked at the face reflected back at him in the large mirror anchored above the sink as he dried his hands on a soft little towel. His long dark hair was a loosely curled mess he had no memory of ever brushing. His features were nice enough but not at all familiar. He glanced downward until his reflection stopped about mid chest, then looked from the mirror to his sculpted body, realizing he must have done something to keep himself in shape.

Seeing himself as if looking for the first time was just weird, and the constant awareness of how every inch of his body felt was...awkward. Everything felt out of place. The feeling of the air on his skin. The weight of his form on his feet. The hollowness of his stomach. Mostly, again, the disjointedness was all he could think about, now he was no longer lost in the fantasy of Rayne Cavanaugh-White's story.

It was more than a little unnerving.

He shook his head, hoping whatever had happened to his memories would straighten themselves out soon.

Able to do nothing but let it go for now, Sabastian walked through the open concept living room and kitchen, broken up by only the kitchen's island and ladder-like stairs leading up toward the loft. The log walls complemented by the décor, or vice versa, gave him a sense of the natural and filled him with a peacefulness thinking didn't. Though minimalist and rustic in many ways, it was obvious great care for the home kept it sparkling clean and looking as if only recently built. The vast array of houseplants and limited furnishings seamlessly flowed to blend in with the forested land just outside the large multi-paned window at the front of the house. Although he had no memories, the setting felt as if it would have always suited him just fine.

"Are you hungry?"

Sabastian turned and looked up to find Celestia

watching him. "Did I wake you?"

She shook her head and made her way to the stairs. He watched as she took them quickly, without even looking down. "Be careful. Those are steep and narrow."

She grinned. "I grew up in this house. I could walk every inch of it with my eyes closed."

He liked seeing the smile on her lips, but then he just liked looking at her. There was an air of delicacy, but strength as well, in her long lithe form and light movements. When she made it to his side, she didn't hesitate to grasp his chin and tilt his head so she could inspect his face. The cool touch of her fingers sent a little jolt through him, and he was certain she felt it when her gaze zoomed to his in concern.

"I'm sorry. Did I hurt you?"

Denial was on his lips but wouldn't pass them as their eyes were once again locked on the other. Both took a deep breath and eased it out slowly then lifted their lips at the same time. Hers in a soft smile and, he feared, his in hunger. She took a step back and turned to the kitchen. Sabastian followed more slowly, hoping he hadn't alarmed her in some way. Deciding he needed to lighten the moment, he settled upon one of the four stools at the bar and waited until she turned back his way. "It would seem I'm attracted to you."

From the way she stared at him, maybe that wasn't the route to take. He grinned. "I don't mean to make you uncomfortable."

Her head shook slightly. "I'm not used to being alone with men I've seen naked."

He could tell by the way she flinched she hadn't meant to say that. But it made him grin. "Are you used to being in public with men you've seen naked?"

The startled eyes, the surprised laughter, and her moving closer was a very satisfying reaction. He enjoyed all three.

"It just so happens I haven't been with any naked men that aren't family." At his brows jumping upward, she laughed again. "That didn't sound right either."

He laughed too. "Not really, no."

Celestia took a deep breath and let it out loudly. He didn't know if she was exasperated at him, or herself. To steer the conversation in a different direction was obviously in order. "So, tell me, where are your parents?"

A guarded look entered her eyes, and he could have kicked himself. "I'm not asking to make sure we are going to remain alone. It was just something to say."

Her lips pressed together as her brows drew closer. "I'm not a very good judge of character," she admitted reluctantly.

Ah... "I'm harmless."

She shrugged, but he could tell it wasn't for his benefit.

"I've had my head in books for most of my adult life." Her words sounded like an apology.

"You must be very smart." She shrugged again, and he could tell no matter what he said, she felt uncomfortable. "If my being here is a problem, I will leave."

A look of distress entered her eyes before she glanced past him. "No. That isn't necessary and not practical right now anyway. It's still snowing and, from the looks of it, has been all day."

Sabastian turned and looked through the large glass window. The world outside was white. Where it not for the snow-free spots of the wood beams holding up the porch roof, it would be nothing but a blinding blur. For some reason, that comforted him.

"It's beautiful."

She smiled slightly and nodded. "It is. But it's also cold and dangerous." Her gaze flittered to the side. "We need to rekindle the fire and then go check on the horses." She glanced back at him. "Would you like a cup of hot tea and something to eat first?"

Sabastian nodded, though he had no idea if he'd like hot tea. He couldn't remember the simplest things, and that bothered him. A lot.

"I'll take care of the fire. Something to eat sounds good."

"You might want to put on some warmer clothes too before we go out. I'll go see what Dad has that will work."

Sabastian nodded as he rubbed his hand across his chest. He hadn't remembered to put on the shirt she'd brought him earlier. Until she'd mentioned it, he hadn't really noticed the chill in the air since she'd entered the room. "That sounds good."

He rose and went to the floor to ceiling rock fireplace. The forethought that went into making wood shelving on either side of it was admirable. Each boxed area filled with cut logs, so it was a simple matter to stoke the glowing coals with more wood. Before long, a nice fire was blazing, and the heat radiating from it felt amazing on his face and exposed skin.

The sounds coming from the kitchen—running water, the clatter of pans and dishes, and the closing of cabinets—filled the cabin as he made his way back to the bedroom he'd occupied all day. The shirt took seconds to retrieve and pull on, although he had to grunt a little through the remaining pain. He looked the room over then made the bed much like it had been before he'd climbed onto it earlier.

"Sabastian?"

Though something about it still felt wrong, the sound of his name on her lips made him smile. He hurried back to front of the cabin to find her setting the island with plates and silverware, as steam rose from two large handled cups. He returned to the seat he'd occupied earlier, and inhaled the scent of something wonderful.

"What are you making?"

Celestia smiled. "Just a quick snack to hold us until we can take care of Cleo and Cleopatra. It's cinnamon biscuits. My mom always made them for us when we were kids so I know the sugar spike will help with our energy levels for the trek to the barn and back. When we get back here, I'll cook the chicken breasts I'm marinating and make a salad."

"That sounds good."

She grinned. "Wait until you taste these. I always thought it was something so special...one because my mom rarely allowed us sweets made with processed sugar growing up, and two, because I had no idea how easy they were to make until I was grown." Her lips twisted. "I'm a fair cook, but nothing like most of the women in my family."

Sabastian studied her lovely features, amazed such a successful and beautiful woman seemed to have such a confidence problem. "You make that sound like it's a big deal. I don't even know if I know how to cook."

The strangeness of the statement made them both smile as their eyes met. And locked. Disappointment filled him when Celestia blinked and looked away immediately, as she blew out a shaky breath.

"The biscuits should be done."

He wanted to reach across the island and take her hands, but she turned from him while pulling on large padded mittens. She opened the door of the stainless steel oven, and the heat rolled at him from around her delectable curves. She closed the door without making a sound, then sat the stone baking sheet with the sparkling mounds on little stands she'd already placed on the counter. A heavenly aroma permeated the air, and Sabastian's mouth literally watered. He swallowed the excess saliva as she lifted biscuits onto their plates, but her attention to detail in placing them at a precise distance made him wonder if she was purposely stalling to keep from looking at him.

"I think, after I help you with the horses, I need to find a way to get out of your hair."

Celestia froze and looked up at him. "That isn't necessary. Really. I'm just not sure what we'll do with each other if we're stuck here for days."

Her pale cheeks pinked prettily, making Sabastian want to caress them. He reached across the island and captured her gloved hands, making her release the spatula as well as the raised lip of the stoneware. She stared at him, her large eyes less frightened than penetrating, as if she was waiting to see what he planned to do. A slow smile pulled at his lips as her nostrils flared delicately.

"You don't need to be afraid of me. I would do nothing you don't want."

****

Celestia swallowed against the fullness in her throat. She had no response. She had no idea what to do with the strange feelings inside her chest. He was without question the most appealing man she'd ever met, but she wasn't in a place to contemplate wanting anything from him. And he wasn't either. He didn't even know who he was....

She pulled back, and her hands slid free of the gloves. His remained where they were, the heat protection now stiffly hanging toward her. She licked lips that held no moisture as he began to lay the gloves on either side of the baking stone. But he stopped mid-motion as his gaze lowered to just below her nose. Celestia waited until his gaze was once again delving into her eyes before speaking.

"You don't know if you're in a relationship. Or married." Her cheeks heated, but she refused to cower and look away. "I mean...."

"Yes. I am captivated by you." He stated. "But you are in charge here."

For some reason that didn't help. The urge to move to him, to touch him, to taste him, was all she could think about doing. It wasn't something she had experienced before. It was something to think on now, but the horses needed attention.

She looked away, at a loss, as the belly hunger she'd awaken with was gone, replaced with what felt like nerves. She cleared her throat. "These are better if we eat them while they're still warm."

Sabastian nodded when she looked his way. "Then sit by me, and let's eat."

Celestia nodded and rounded the island, leaving a stool between them when she sat. She pulled her plate closer and stared at the aromatic biscuits, but was afraid she'd choke if she placed one between her lips. She lifted her cup instead, fully aware he'd yet to touch his own nourishment. After blowing, she took a sip, and then slid her gaze to meet his.

"You aren't eating."

Sabastian's lips rose slightly. "I was waiting for you."

She lowered the cup slightly and let the moist heat rise to bathe her face. "I didn't poison them."

"Never thought you did."

She grinned slightly. "I'm out of sorts today."

He nodded as his brows drew together. "It's been an interesting one, that's for sure."

"I don't usually sleep the day away."

"You were exhausted."

She nodded. "I was."

"I'm sorry to be such a burden."

Ashamed to have made him feel that way, she shook her head. "You aren't a burden. Just a…surprise."

"I haven't thanked you for saving me."

"There's no need. I'm sure you would have done the same."

"Thanks, anyway. And I guess I would have. I don't

know."

Silence filled the space around them. Celestia figured he was as lost in thought as he was lost in every other way. She took a sip of her tea and enjoyed its slow slide down her throat. She lifted her napkin to wipe her lips, only then realizing how rough and chapped they were. It was no wonder. She'd been out in the cold for more hours than she could count.

"I'm not married."

She sent him a surprised look. That was the last thing she would have thought on his mind. "How would you know?"

He shrugged and tore off a piece of biscuit before placing it into his mouth. He chewed thoughtfully for several seconds before swallowing and turning back her way. "I feel like I'm not."

Celestia didn't know why that made her smile. But it did. "What *do* you feel like?"

Sabastian took a sip of his tea then looked at her in surprise. "This is good."

"A family blend. Dried out by my mother, from the indigenous plants growing here on the mountain."

He nodded but didn't ask the usual next question: was Haven Cavanaugh-Hansen a farmer, herbalist, or actual tea manufacturer. Over the years, there had been many questions from the fellow students and future colleagues, invited to her apartment to complete the group assignment requirements she'd always hated. She'd preferred to work alone then as she did now, but college was college and people were nosy. Because of that, it was rare she'd invited anyone over.

Part of it was her discomfort with people in general, and part was an ingrained sense of self-preservation all the Cavanaughs grew up learning to live by. Ultimately, the students all asked the one question she could never answer:

'What kind of plants were used in the blend?' which was more often than not, followed up by: 'Is this stuff legal?' since the tea held properties that lifted the spirit and restored the body, in ways individual to the drinker's need. She'd passed off answering with a smile and a partial truth, saying it was as a family secret. Some had been gracious about accepting her response, others not so much. Even those pushier ones she gave a pass to, because they were all into science. And scientists were always thirsty for answers.

"I don't know… I just feel like I would know if I was married. Or loved someone. I don't think I ever have."

Drawn back to the present, she mulled his words over. It was an interesting thing to say, and something she would have found suspect if not for his casual sincerity. He sounded as if was testing the words out for himself rather than trying to convince her. "I've never been in love."

Why that popped out was beyond her, but the interested look in his eyes wasn't the response she needed. She focused on the cooling biscuits in front of her and lifted one to take a bite. If nothing else, it would keep her from making another stupid comment.

"I wish you'd relax."

Celestia closed her eyes, wishing she could too. But being near him, inhaling his scent, and sharing a meal, meager as it was, was sending her into sensory overload. She smiled at him anyway, hoping it looked sincere. "Okay." She took a cleansing breath and blew it out. "Eat up, and let's get geared up so we can get to the horses."

She followed his gaze to realize his plate was empty. "Oh. Do you want more?"

He shook his head and stood. "No, thanks. You finish up, and I'll meet you at the back door."

Celestia nodded and quickly ate only one of her biscuits, drank her tepid tea, and made a dash for the bathroom, before climbing to the loft to find him something more substantial to wear. The snow would be high by now, she was sure, and the T-shirt and sweats she'd given him weren't likely to do much in the way of protection.

Though, for the life of her, she couldn't figure out why he was the one in need of protection.

Chapter Five

Sabastian's back was to her when she entered the small mudroom, his hands holding the short curtains open as he peered out the window into the back yard. She took a moment to admire the silky loose deep brown curls, and the broad shoulders they just passed. The memory of the muscle playing down his tapered back when he'd been shirtless earlier, the tight rounded butt and long legs now encased in the sweats, sent her heart into overtime. As if sensing her presence he dropped the curtains and turned slowly.

"It's going to be deep."

Celestia nodded, hoping she hadn't gotten caught ogling him. If so, he was too much of a gentleman to let it show. "I figured it would be. I know you were exposed for a long time, if you don't feel up to going with me, I can handle his."

Disbelief flashed across his features. "You think I would let you go out there alone?"

She shrugged. "I would have had to if you hadn't shown up, or if your injuries had been worse."

"I did show up. And I'm fine."

Not certain why he looked and sounded annoyed, Celestia held up the clothing she'd chosen. "I hope these will fit you. My dad isn't as tall as you are. I think Mom said he's six one, and you have to be at least three or four inches taller. There are socks and another shirt folded in the jeans for you to put on too. I know Dad, and my mom, have thermal underwear around here somewhere, but I guess she hasn't gotten out their winter gear yet. It's probably in the building out back… I don't think we've ever had this bad a snowstorm so early in the season," Celestia finished helplessly, pinned by the hunger in his sparkling gaze.

Sabastian took the bundle from her hands. He lifted his right hand to run a finger across her lower lip, as he studied her mouth. "They will be fine, I'm sure. Thank you. You need to put something on your lips to protect them."

Celestia took a step back and glanced around the small mudroom just so she didn't have to look into his eyes. She knew her reaction to his touch was foolish. She was an adult woman. He was an attractive man. Beginning and end of story. There was no reason for her to make more of it than it was. She glanced back up to find him silently studying her.

He had a sense of stillness about him that should have been comfortable since she wasn't a fidgety person either. But his calm, like everything else about him, was taking up her oxygen as well as her thoughts. She'd never had so much trouble getting enough air into her lungs before but now found the need to take great gulps regularly.

"Go ahead and get dressed and pick out a pair of boots," she said, pointing to those sitting within the cubbies below the padded bench, which was located beneath the coat hooks. "Hopefully Dad's will be close to your size. I'll be back in a few minutes. I'm going to pack us some supplies. Just in case we need them. You never take chances of being unprepared on this mountain when it snows… and like I said, I don't remember it ever snowing like this."

She grabbed the backpack her mother always kept handy for the long walks she and Celestia's father took through the woods and went into the kitchen. Bottled water manufactured at the base of the mountain by her uncle's tribe was a given, so those went in first. Not only was it pure refreshment, the water came straight from within the mountain, and held magical properties that strengthened those mystics lucky enough to consume it. As far as she knew, other than her cousin Dia's lover, there was no evidence those vacationers who'd rented Tom Whitehawk's cabins in the spring, summer and fall, had been affected in any way, even though the same water was piped into all the cabins on the mountain.

Next, she scooped enough of her mother's trail mix into a small container. The berries, edible dried flower petals, and cinnamon-soaked little balls of oats were her mother's concoction and locally acquired, with only the variety of nuts coming from outside the vast grounds around their home. Homemade flatbread baked by her mother and cheese produced from one of uncle Tom's goats was added on a whim, along with grapes, a couple of apples for the horses, and the small tangerines that were her personal favorite.

Celestia spotted her father's culinary claim to fame covered beneath a glass dome in the back of the refrigerator, and it took all she had not to cut them both a slice of the rich chocolate-on-chocolate-on-chocolate cake.

They could have that later.

Smiling at the expected moans of pleasure eating the delicious treat would bring to her lips, and she was certain to Sabastian's, she closed the refrigerator door, turned with her booty, and jumped back. Sabastian was standing there, a grin on his lips.

"Are we planning to run away for good?"

Celestia felt her cheeks heat. "I'm making us a survival kit."

"Is the barn that far away?"

She moved past him to lay the food on the island, next to the backpack. "No. Not normally. But if that snow is as deep as it looks, we are going to have a time getting there and back."

"I could go alone."

Celestia shook her head. "No. The animals are my responsibility." She looked him over. With the flannel shirt's sleeves unbuttoned and obviously too short, and jeans that stopped just above the ankle, he looked ridiculous and cute at the same time. For some reason that eased the tension of being in his presence. "Looks like Dad's clothes are too small."

He grinned. "The clothes will do. I tried on a pair of boots. They'll work too."

Celestia finished packing their food supplies after adding in a couple of more apples. "We'll take a blanket too. Mom keeps one in the bench in the mudroom that will protect us from the elements should we get stuck out there. It's meant for people who hike in extreme conditions."

Sabastian nodded. "You're really worried about this."

"No, not really. It's just better to be safe than sorry."

"Tell me what I can do to help."

Celestia smiled. "Just promise me you really are okay before we head out there. I don't think I can carry you back if you decided to pass out on me."

Sabastian reached up, touched his temple and then nodded. "I feel great actually."

The surprise in his voice was reassuring. It meant he wasn't trying to convince her but really was okay. "Then let's finish preparing and go make sure the horses are okay."

He picked up the backpack before she could do it herself and headed to the mudroom. It took only seconds to find the rolled blanket, which she attached to the backpack's strings. They both pulled on high boots, the heaviest jackets her parents owned, and scarves and gloves as well, once she realized they'd need them.

"Ready?"

Sabastian, looking twice his normal girth and bundled-up like a swaddled baby, grinned at her.

"Ready."

Opening the back door, in, was easy. Trying to push the screen door against the snow that was on the other side of it took effort. She stepped back when Sabastian touched her arm and allowed him to wrestle the door until the snow swept back enough so they could step through. She didn't object when he took the first step into the deeper snow, only followed in his high steps as he moved forward.

"We'll have to get some shovels from the garage on our way back. This is ridiculous."

Sabastian turned back to her and nodded. "I see what you mean now. Even making it to the garage is going to be difficult. The snow is nearly to my knees. Just how far away is the barn?"

"It's just around behind those trees over there." She pointed at the barely visible distant tree line, and when he turned back to her with raised brows, she knew exactly how he felt. "But we have to pass a pond first. I just hope we can make out the banks and don't fall in. I don't think it's cold enough to have frozen over yet."

The realization her mother could easily eliminate the snow with a swipe of her hand wasn't lost on her. Haven Cavanaugh-Hanson was the equivalent of Mother Nature and could manipulate the elements with little thought. Were her great-aunt Lune Brille Cavanaugh available and not somewhere off in an exotic location, she would be equally as handy, since she was that generation's elemental mystic. But neither was here, and Dia, the most recent generation with that particular gift, probably was too taken with the new discovery of her pregnancy to realize she had the same powers as well. If only there was some way to know what was going on....

"I wish Mom had left a charger here for my cell phone. At least then I could have made contact with the rest of the family to see if everyone is okay."

Sabastian peered back at her. Only his snow-tipped dark lashes and watering eyes were visible from within the mounting snow atop the scarf. She hadn't realized until then his taking the lead also meant he took the brunt of wind and weather. "It's picking up again. Maybe we should go back to the house."

Sabastian's eyelids crinkled, and she could tell he was smiling. "Oh, so you don't like this? It's almost magical. Don't you think?"

Celestia couldn't help but grin back at his choice of words. If only he knew, the mountain really was filled with magic, both itself and its occupants! But of course, she couldn't say that. "If you discount that fact we might freeze to death."

Concern entered his eyes. "Are you cold?"

Giving it some thought, she shook her head. "Not really. I'm pretty bundled up and we're working just by walking, but we haven't been out here that long yet either."

Sabastian nodded. "We're almost to the garage. I don't supposed there's anything in there we could ride?"

Since there was, and it hadn't occurred to her, she felt silly. "Actually there is. Dad has a tractor he uses to mow, but there's a scoop attachment too. The problem is I'm not sure how to drive it. It's been years since I rode on the fender with my dad driving."

"Let's check it out. If we can figure it out, it would save us both a lot of time and effort."

"That's a great idea. Let's go."

Given the excitement she felt, the next five minutes of high stepping to make it to the garage was nothing. Blessing her father's heart, she found the entry door on the far left of the building was unlocked and the interior was not nearly as cold. They were now out of the wind and falling snow, and Celestia knocked the mound of flakes from her shoulders and took her scarf off to shake it out. Sabastian did the same as he looked around the large building filled with both work and play equipment.

The tractor was at the far end with its attachments lined up to its right. A variety of four-wheelers, a motorcycle, and a fishing boat were arranged for easy access, behind the second of the two large garage doors. And before them was an open floor space with a lift built in. Behind the area, where her father would pretend to work on his equipment, were several large drawers that held the tools his surgeon's hands rarely touched.

Sabastian slid her a glance. "Your father has quite a place here. This is a great shop. I hope we don't break anything."

Celestia shrugged. "It looks more intimidating than it is. Daddy likes to pretend he can fix his equipment when something goes wrong. But the truth is, the tools are probably still in their packaging. My dad is a doctor...a surgeon actually. Those hands don't work on anything other than human hearts for the most part. If the drawers on those chests have ever been opened, I'd say my uncles were the ones to do so."

Sabastian laughed. "I have no idea what to do with any of it, so I can't say a word."

Celestia bit her bottom lip. There was so much she wanted to know about Sabastian but didn't want to poke and prod his mind when it was clear he had no answers to her questions. It wasn't as if he was acting shady or secretive. In fact, he seemed completely without guile, a refreshing change from her limited experience in the dating pool. But also frustrating.

She didn't want to like him too much. Just being attracted to him was enough of a problem. He didn't know anything about his life, and hers was in transition. Were it not for the snow, she would even now be moving from her house, into the apartment over her new practice. She knew none of the family understood her need to move, but she'd been having...visions? No, that wasn't the right word. It was more a feeling she was being watched, when no one else was around.

A part of her had wanted to say something to her family about it. Another part, the one that made her fear something was wrong with her mind, had kept her from doing so. They were all so busy with the normal things... if one could call anything that happened to her family members normal.

Her parents, aunts and uncles were across the country handling whatever was happening to her cousin Gavin. And for the last few year's they'd had to deal with so much. Her cousin Jewell had been drawn back in time into an ancient Egyptian body of a mischievous princess. Her cousin Sapphire had been at such risk, infected with more than just the Lycanthrope strain that nearly took her life. And *their* youngest sister Diamond was only just now beginning to recover from the magical mishaps that had happened to her. Her own baby sister Luna even now was transformed into a creature none before had believed existed.

Being a part of the Cavanaugh clan was as confusing as it was joyful. She knew she shouldn't worry over whatever it was going on in her head, since it was likely the manifestation of her powers finally coming in to being, but she couldn't help but wonder if it was something else. Something physical...something medical. Of course, if that were the case she would eventually have to tell her mother. But if the matriarch healer of the family found it was not something she could heal, then she'd worry everyone over something beyond their vast control. There was no way she could go to a physician outside of the family. One blood test and all hell would break loose. For them all.

"Celestia?"

"Huh?"

"Celestia? Are you okay?"

Celestia took a deep breath and blew out stream in the cold air. "I'm sorry. What?"

Sabastian moved closer and looked her over. "You look pale."

Celestia laughed it off. "I always look pale. It comes with being born with white hair."

Sabastian's brows pulled together. "Does everyone in your family look like you?"

That was an interesting question. She'd been born with the exactly same DNA as her siblings. But unlike three millennia of generations of Cavanaughs before, who looked exactly alike, she looked nothing like her sisters. Modern science would fly right out the window if the three of them were ever tested for their genetic makeup now. According to her mother, following their births, their doctor was thrown into a panic, and the poor guy spent the rest of his life trying to prove they were actually monozygotic triplets rather than the polyzygotic siblings they appeared to be. "No. My next younger sister is a brunette, and the youngest a redhead."

"Oh."

Celestia took in the confusion in his eyes. "Why do you ask?"

He shivered as if a chill ran through him. "I don't know... It's strange, but I...I don't know." He rubbed his hand across his forehead then placed three fingers on the area where he'd hit his head. "I guess I hit my head hard. For some reason something struck me as odd, but I couldn't grasp the thought before it was gone."

Moving closer, Celestia took his hand and moved it from his temple. The connection was jolting, but she tried to ignore that as she inspected the wound. Since it seemed fine, short of the bruising and the scrapes, she looked back into his eyes. They too looked fine, discounting the fact he was once again searching hers before his gaze dropped to her lips. Celestia took a shaky breath and stepped back. "Let's see if we can figure out how to work the tractor."

She didn't wait for a response but immediately went to the large green farming implement, which her father kept as clean as one would a shiny new car. The single step was high, and she yelped when she felt Sabastian's hand pushing upward against her bottom. Celestia looked back at him in surprise. Only to find a slight grin on his lips.

"I'm just trying to help."

Celestia bit her lip to keep from smiling. Nor did she form the reprimand she didn't feel like uttering even though she knew she should. Instead, she swung her leg over the hump between the seat and long shifter, settled, and sent a silent thanks to her father again. The key was in the starter. She pointed to the panel beside the large garage door she faced. "Push that top button, and let's see if I can get this thing out of here." She glanced down to find him staring at her, instead of moving to do as she asked. When he continued to watch her, she added a, "Please?"

As if being awakened, Sabastian nodded once and worked his way across the front of the tractor. One touch of his finger, and the motor above her head kicked on and began wrapping the chain as the door rose. Immediately the wind and snow hit her full in the face. And him too, apparently, as he scrambled back to step up at her side.

"Do you want to drive it? Or do you want me to give it a try?"

Thinking of the vast array of males in her life, father, uncles, cousins and cousins by marriage, she knew what kind of relationship they all had with anything automotive. She grinned at him and swung her leg over to settle on the strip of steel that covered the large tire. "You hop on."

It took only seconds, and Sabastian was in the bouncing seat and looking over the panel of gauges before him. He pointed at one then touched another, before he pulled his scarf up on his head and turned to her. "Bundle up. This is going to be fun."

He gave her only a moment before he turned the key and ground the shifter into the clearly marked first gear. The tractor jumped, threw them both back and died. Sabastian caught her before she fell off the back, the waited until she settled again.

"I think you have to push in that pedal and lift it slowly while you push on that one over there," she said, pointing to both clutch and fuel pedal.

Sabastian nodded. "Okay. Sorry."

"Don't worry about it. It's all just now coming back to me." She pointed to the clutch again. "Push that one down and hold it until you are ready to put it in gear and move forward. Then lift your foot slowly."

He nodded again, this time more cautious, doing as instructed. They inched forward, the tractor jerked, and he hit the fuel pedal harder. Celestia held on to his shoulder this time and ducked with him as they moved forward enough to get the nose of the tractor out of the barn.

"Okay! Stop!"

Sabastian lifted his foot immediately and the tractor jerked, coughed, and died, before it started rolling backward. "Put your foot on the brake," Celestia barked, then spun around to jump down. Her feet hit the concrete floor hard, and pain sprang up her right leg. She ignored it as she reached over and threw the hand brake into place, before looking up to see dread on Sabastian's face. A deep calming breath gave her back equilibrium, and she grinned up at him. "You did pretty good."

The surprise flashing in his eyes made her smile fully. That was a mistake. Her already cracked lips felt like they split completely open. She placed her gloved fingers over them, wishing she'd remembered to put lip balm in their survival pack.

"I'm sorry. I guess this isn't as easy as it looks."

"Don't worry about it." She lowered her hand. "I'm afraid this is pretty much a case of the blind leading the blind. I used to ride with my dad sometimes when I was little, but I guess I'd forgotten a lot of what needs to happen, until after we got it wrong. At least you have it out enough we can roll the scraper shovel over here and prepare to attach it to the front once we get the tractor turned around. After that, it should be easy-peasy!"

Sabastian sent her a doubtful look as he climbed down from the tractor and walked to the piece of equipment they needed. Thankfully, her father kept everything accessible and the heavier implements on specially built dollies so they didn't have to worry about dragging the large steel blade to get it into place. She grasped one top corner, and he the other, and they swung it around and placed the connector bars facing outward. Sabastian looked up, a brow raised.

"You want to move the tractor, or give me another try at it?"

"You. Only this time, we'll go over everything I now remember. We just have to be careful. There is real danger in not handling all this right."

He glanced down at the blade. "How about you turn it around and I attach it? Then we can figure the rest out from there?"

Celestia nodded. It made more sense for him to do the heavy work once she took care of the practical. She walked past him to the assortment of toolboxes and only had to open three neatly filled drawers before she came upon the one with assorted sizes of the heavy-duty pins and clips they'd need to secure everything together.

She returned to Sabastian and handed everything over, then grasped one of the two bars that would attach to the tractor. "When I get the tractor in position, I'll lower the braces. Its holes will need to align with these," she said, sticking her finger in one. "Slide the big pins in, and then use the little ones to slide into these holes. Once we get both sides attached, we'll be ready to go."

Sabastian nodded. "Looks simple enough."

Celestia smiled as she glanced up at him. "As long as you don't pinch or smash a finger."

"I'll be careful. You do the same."

With nothing left to say, Celestia tightened her scarf around her neck, hoping the thin layer of protection would keep her head warm enough for however long this little chore demanded. As it was, she was worried they'd taken too much time preparing to care for the horses than actually caring for them.

Much to her relief, the workings of the tractor, since she finally remembered all she'd learned when she was younger, was a piece of cake. The tires slipped a couple of times over the wet snow when she started. But that was because she tried to take off too quickly. That lesson learned, she allowed the tractor to crawl at its own pace until she completely cleared the garage and then gave it only a little fuel as she made the wide turn taking her back. There was one hesitant moment as she inched close to the building's open door, but she rode the brake until she was right between the bars. Taking the tractor out of gear, she set the brake and smiled at Sabastian in triumph.

As he'd smartly kept clear of her entry, Sabastian's smile stayed in place as he moved forward. He glanced down as she engaged the lift just enough that her bars were right below the blade's bars.

"Pull them wide just a little," she said, and he did.

The assembly was quickly completed. Her confidence they would get to the horses rose several degrees.

"You look really cute up there."

Celestia's smile faltered and she exhaled a shaky breath.

"Thank you."

His smile slid. "Why do you look so defensive when someone compliments you? Or is it just me you're afraid of?"

"I'm not afraid of you." The words felt like a lie. Celestia shrugged. "I guess maybe I am a little. But not that you'll hurt me. You would've already done that if it was your intent."

He studied her. "Then why?"

Not able to maintain eye contact, she looked over the gauges on the dashboard. "I'm not afraid...maybe just uncomfortable."

"Because?"

Her gaze fluttered back to his. Was he really going to make her admit it? If the slight smile lifting his lips and making his eyes twinkle was any indication, he already knew the answer.

"You are a man, a stranger, and I am a woman, and we're alone."

"I told you I wouldn't do anything you didn't want."

That was the problem. Her discomfort level with him was because it felt too comfortable to be with him, so her attraction to him wasn't purely physical. If that had been the case, she could have easily dismissed it. "I like you."

His head tilted as he stared at her. There was no playfulness in the deep penetrating gaze.

"I like you, too."

Celestia didn't know why she'd said the words, and now that he'd said them back, it felt too complicated to continue talking. "Well, we'd better get going. Do you want to drive?"

Sabastian shook his head. "No, it looks like you've got it down. I'll ride on the fender."

She ran her hand across the metal to wipe off the snow that had covered it then waited while he climbed on. Once he settled, she threw the tractor into reverse and backed out slowly. Once the blade was clear of the building, she pressed the remote her father had fortunately placed in the cubby and watched as the garage door slid closed.

"That's handy."

Celestia grinned from behind her scarf. "Something else I belatedly remembered. My dad likes his conveniences."

"Smart man."

More relaxed talking about something other than themselves, she backed enough she could safely turn and headed the tractor past the barn and into the open field. The problem was, with so much snow, she wasn't sure how near they were to the pond. Celestia purposely stayed as close to what her mother considered the back yard as she could, until they reached the tree line. Certain she'd eliminated any chance of driving into the water, she relaxed and glanced his way.

Sabastian was looking forward but must have sensed her gaze as his head swung around so he could look behind them, then his eyes settled on hers.

"This is beautiful, but I'm glad we're riding. That snow is several inches deep."

She took a quick second to glance back at the deep tracks the tractor made, and nodded. "Me, too. We'd have barely gotten anywhere by now on foot. At the rate we're going, we should get to the opening in the trees shortly, and the barn is just a little ways on the other side."

A strong gust of wind hit Celestia in the face, making the snowflakes dance and mounds plop from the nearby trees. "Looks like the winds are shifting."

Sabastian's eyes weren't on her, but rather he was looking over her head. She glanced over to see what had put the concern in his eyes, and a chill ran down her spine. The already grey sky was darkening as what looked like a thick blanket of clouds headed their way. It appeared the clouds brought a wall of heavier snow with them, so she increased the tractor's speed, hoping they made it to the barn before the onslaught arrived.

Celestia kept her focus on their destination, again wishing she could contact her mother or, at this point, any member of the family. There was something strange about the clouds coming at them, and it chilled her even more than the snow penetrating her jeans.

Chapter Six

Sabastian jumped from the tractor as soon as they pulled inside the barn. Celestia breathed a sigh of relief. She too was ready to get down and shake off the snow. She braked and turned off the motor as Sabastian wrestled the large doors closed, throwing the barn into darkness.

"There's a light switch to your left. Would you flip it on, please?"

The barn immediately bathed in soft white lights. Being out of the chilly wind was such a relief. Though frozen to the bone, Celestia scrambled to get down and was thrilled to welcome Cleo as he came to her. If nothing else, his welcoming nudge warmed her heart.

"It's a mess out there, boy. Are you and Cleopatra okay?"

His head bobbed up and down, making her smile.

"He's beautiful."

Celestia turned back to find Sabastian looking at her and Cleo. His gaze slid past them and, as his scarf fell away, a brighter smile filled his face. He skirted them both and headed straight for Cleopatra's stall. Without hesitation, they stood there nuzzling each other.

The filly whinnied endearingly, and though his voice was too low for her to make out the words, Celestia was certain Sabastian was praising the white beauty. She grinned at Cleo. "Looks like you have some competition, my friend."

Cleo glanced over his shoulder so he could look back, and then he turned to Celestia and shook his large head. Since his eyes held more than a little annoyance, she laughed, and kissed his jaw. "Don't worry about it. You know you have Cleopatra's heart."

Celestia ran her hand down his neck, then over his high back as she made her way to man and mare. Sabastian turned to her with such a big grin she couldn't help but smile back. Since her own heart belonged to the animals of the world, his affection for the horse only touched her more.

"Let's get them covered with their blankets and then clean out their stalls. The straw is up there," she said, pointing to the loft. "Dad has made this all so easy, we should have them bedded and fed in no time at all."

"It's so cold in here. Are you sure they'll be okay?"

Celestia nodded. "Once we turn on the heat and take care of them, yes. I should have done it this morning."

His eyes lost their shine. "You were a little busy taking care of me." He turned back to Cleopatra and rubbed her jaw. "I'm sorry, baby."

Celestia watched as they snuggled a little more before he opened the door and stepped inside. "I'll start cleaning hers. It looks like she needs more oats." He peered out at Celestia. "Can we get them fresh water?"

She nodded. "Yes. The water is piped in from the mountain into each stall, and to a deep sink in the tack room. Dad had the pipes wrapped when he had them installed, and it isn't cold enough for freezing to be of much concern, at least not once it warms up in here." She headed to the thermostat and turned it to heat, thankful her father had the electric heating added when they'd first brought the horse home. The other upgrades to the already snuggly built barn were added then as well, for the horses' comfort and care. Were it not for her parents' kindness, she had no idea where she would have housed the two once she'd saved them from their neglectful owner.

Celestia returned to him and pointed to the slatted wall

that separated the stalls. "There's a spigot in the corner closest to Cleo's stall that shares the same plumbing. The pitchforks and wheelbarrows are in the tool shed just past Cleo's stall along with their brushes, shampoos, and other supplies. If you want to go on and start cleaning a stall out, I'll climb up and drop bales down so we can spread the bedding out once everything is ready. Then we'll take care of food and water."

"Sounds good. Is it okay if she comes out while I do it?"

Celestia smiled, truly enjoying his concern for the animal. "Sure. The doors are closed. She isn't going anywhere."

Thinking Cleopatra wasn't likely to leave Sabastian anyway, she watched as the mare walked regally from her stall, stopping only long enough to nudge Sabastian before making her way to show Cleo she held as much affection for him. Celestia grinned when the horse glanced her way, and she could have sworn the beautiful creature winked at her.

It had been months since she'd climbed the ladder going up to the loft, but as always, her parents kept everything neat and tidy. The straw was stacked and packed tightly, and there was enough that they'd make it through the remaining fall months and winter without issue. Even though they hadn't expected the early snowstorm, her family knew to prepare for the worst when it came to weather conditions. And it looked like this year was going to trump all those that came before.

The same over-the-top preparations were made regarding the alfalfa supply, with only the oats and vitamins something they would purchase on an ongoing, as needed, basis. Because her parents had wanted to help by taking care of the horses' everyday needs since the rescue, Celestia hadn't had to lift the heavy bales until now, and it reminded her of just how long it had been since she'd done anything so physical. If she discounted getting the gorgeous man down below to the house this morning.

Was it really just this morning?

It was a little disorienting to remember she'd only just met him. But that was probably due to sleep-depravation overriding the daylong nap she'd taken. She had only done all-nighters while studying for big tests. She never slept during the day. Now both were messing with her senses.

The darkness of the loft reminded her night fell earlier every day this time of year, and that would only make it more dangerous for them when they headed back to the cabin. With a growing sense of urgency, she maneuvered eight bales to the edge of the loft and then looked down. No doubt knowing the ropes, Cleo and Cleopatra were waiting and watching from the far end of the bar and were out of harm's way. Sabastian was probably not so informed. "Look out below!"

"I'm clear!"

Sabastian's quick response made her smile and wonder if his affinity with the animals was an indication some had played a large role in the life he couldn't remember. But with so much at stake, she didn't have time to ponder. She pushed the first bale off and leaned over enough to watch it hit the concrete floor and bounce, as loose pieces of straw flew out and rolled a couple of times before settling.

"Bale number two coming down!"

She repeated the process for each bale, sending out the forewarning every time. Once the last one landed in what had become a haphazard pile, she turned back to the ladder. "I'm coming down!"

It was a relief her father had the forethought to extend the ladder's frame and rungs up into the loft so she didn't have to awkwardly turn and step down through the opening without hand supports. But her father was a thoughtful man in everything he did and had more than likely designed the barn with her mother's comforts in mind. Not that her mother would bother with a ladder. Haven Cavanaugh-White would likely zap herself up or zap the bales down and then make them spread themselves with a flick of her magical hand. The thought that her mother would also send brooms dancing to clean up the mess when all was said and done made Celestia smile.

She backed down the ladder so swiftly her right boot slipped from the next rung. Before she could reconnect, hands cupped her hips and lifted her down. She glanced back into Sabastian's terrified eyes.

"I didn't want you to fall."

"I don't think I would have."

"You have to be careful!"

His words were tense, as was the seriousness of his gaze.

"What's wrong?"

He shook his head slightly while his brows drew together. "I don't know... When your foot slipped, I felt like I was the one falling. I'm not sure...but I think I might have fallen out of the sky."

Horror smacked Celestia in the chest. "You mean from an airplane?"

He looked so lost and confused Celestia wrapped her arms around his chest and pulled him into a hug. "I guess it's possible," she said slowly. "People have survived being ejected from planes. I've heard of people who fell into trees and survived. And it would explain you being all scratched and bruised in the middle of a forest, on this mountain. But why would you have been naked?"

"I don't know."

She pulled back and looked up into his face. "Do you remember being on an airplane? Or falling? Or anything?"

He was so still Celestia knew he was trying to recall,

but he finally shook his head. "No. Not a memory. Just that fleeting second of feeling. As soon as I touched you, it was gone."

She stepped back and ran her hands over his arms to both thaw her frozen fingers and warm him. "Maybe it means your memories are trying to return." Frustration made her press her lips together. "If I could just contact someone…anyone, then we could find out if you were reported missing, or if there was an aviation accident report, or something that would help."

"I know."

She took another step back. "Let's get this done and see if it looks safe for us to return to the cabin. I was sure my mother had a charger that would fit my phone. It has to be there somewhere."

Sabastian nodded and returned to Cleopatra's stall. Celestia retrieved a second wheelbarrow and pitchfork and went into Cleo's stall. Within minutes, Sabastian joined her and they worked together to collect the soiled straw. He said nothing, and neither did she. She was certain they were both too deep in thought about their predicaments to converse.

After the last pile was forked and loaded, Sabastian turned to take the wheelbarrow out of the stall to sit it beside the one he'd already filled. "Where do I take these?"

Celestia rubbed her hands together, certain they were not only chapped now but had blisters beneath her gloves. "Dad keeps a wagon out that door," she said, pointing toward the one leading to the woods. "It's probably covered with snow, but we can fork this mess on top of it anyway."

"I'll do that if you want to take care of the water."

Thankful he was such a gentleman, Celestia nodded. "Thank you. I really don't know how well I would have done all this on my own."

His lips lifted. "You're welcome. I'll just be a few minutes. Then we'll get them fed and bedded."

She watched as he took the first wheelbarrow of muck to the doors then returned for the second before opening the door and letting in the cold. She stepped inside the stall closest to her. The remaining water in the trough had a thin coat of ice over it but adding more took care of that. With the heat on, she wouldn't have to worry about them or their water freezing. She let it run while starting Cleopatra's, then went back and waited until it was full enough to turn off.

She heard the other being turned off as well and realized Sabastian had returned. They stepped from each stall at the same time and grinned at each other.

"Thanks again for handling that. Now we need to carry the straw in and cut the strings so we can spread it all out."

"I can do that too. You look tired."

That was not exactly something a woman wanted to hear from an attractive man, but the truth was she was tired and still chilled and wanted nothing more than to get back to the cabin and sit in front of the fire. "I'm fine." She lied. "Let's get this done."

He nodded and carried six bales in to her four, and then they worked together to unbind and spread the straw. Celestia looked around when they were finished, wondering... "I think we should add another bale to each stall in case we aren't able to get back for a while. Maybe double or triple their rations too. Just to be on the safe side. And if we leave their stall doors open, it's less likely they'll soil them. I'd be happy to clean the barn up later. What do you think?"

Sabastian smiled at her. "I think you know a lot more than I do about all this, so you just tell me what you need me to do and it's done."

It was so strange to have someone to work with. She'd

always preferred to be alone with her studies and her life in general. But this was so much better, especially since Sabastian was the one whose company she kept. She appreciated everything about him. His kind nature, his love of animals, and yes, the fact he was such a pleasure to look at. Realizing she was staring at him, she looked away.

"Celestia?"

Unexpected bashfulness made it difficult to look back into his eyes, but she forced herself to anyway. He moved closer. Her breath caught and held as he stopped and lifted his hands to push back a strand of hair. She waited, as anticipation sent a shiver down her spine that had nothing at all to do with the cold. Then she felt foolish when he pulled out straw and held it up for her to see. She reached up and placed her palms over his when he went for more, only to find herself captured by them both. His head lowered and his lips lightly brushed hers.

One taste turned into two, then a third, before he eased back to look into her eyes. "You didn't tell me to stop."

She shook her head slowly. "No. I didn't."

His lips spread into a satisfied smile before they took hers again. Celestia let her inhibitions go and kissed him back, enjoying the leisurely exploration. He seemed in no hurry to deepen it as her previous dates had when she'd allowed a goodnight kiss. When he finally lifted his head, hers was reeling with want.

It wasn't until Sabastian released her and stepped back that she noticed the wind whistling around the barn.

"I think we should get the horses taken care of quickly."

She nodded. "Yes. You're right. I'm already concerned about getting back to the cabin in the dark. The tractor has headlights, but I don't think they'll be much help if it's snowing hard."

Although the lower part of the barn had lost much of the earlier chill, she couldn't make it too warm on the horses so she'd only set it for sixty-eight degrees. They'd be worse off if they began sweating and then became chilled, than if their ability to regulate their bodies naturally came into play. But as chilled as she was, that wouldn't be enough to warm her stiffening bones. And after his earlier experience, she was afraid it even worse for Sabastian.

"Let's get them fed," she said, and headed to the shed where her parents had the still strong smelling green bales stored. Unlike straw, which was nothing more than dried wheat stalks and had no nutritional value, the clover and alfalfa mix would not only fill the animal's stomachs with bulk, it would add needed nutrients to their diet. And, although there were also large round bales of hay made from the acres of grasses her father had cut over the spring and summer lined and stacked just a quarter of a mile beyond the barn, the horses would always get the best nature had to offer, as she and her family would have it no other way.

Celestia climbed up the natural steps the staggered bales made, and told Sabastian to wait below so she could throw down those on top first. Once she lifted each and pitched it down, he carried them by twos over to stack outside of the stalls. She climbed down and followed him back as he carried the last load, and they again cut the twine and loaded the open-barred feeders purchased to keep the food separate from the straw covering the floor. Now that the harder parts of her chores were complete, they gave each horse a triple scoop of oats in their cloth buckets, and stood back as the horses reentered their stalls.

Celestia kissed Cleo on the jaw and saw Sabastian doing the same with Cleopatra. Smiling she stepped back and looked at them both. "You two stay warm. I'll try to get back tomorrow."

"We."

She glanced over at Sabastian and nodded. "Yes. We."

Cleo nodded his large head up and down. Cleopatra again nudged Sabastian, Celestia supposed, in farewell.

She headed to the tractor as Sabastian went to the large doors. "Would you like something to drink first?"

Sabastian stopped and looked back, his eyes thoughtful, before he nodded and heading to her. Celestia pulled out their survival pack, hoping they'd both be able to hydrate quickly and get back to the cabin without delay. The rising whistling wind-sounds coming from outside of the barn were worrisome, but she didn't want to burden him with her concerns.

He nearly downed the bottle of water in one gulp, finishing off the remainder seconds later. Celestia didn't waste time drinking hers either, though she didn't usually act in such an unladylike manner. She lowered the bottle and took his before returning them to the backpack. "Do you want more? Or are you ready to go?"

"Ready."

His short reply confirmed her fear they'd kept him out too long, and he'd probably done more than he should have, given the frightening possibility Sabastian had actually fallen from an airplane. She could only hope, once those large barn doors were open, he'd be well enough to handle the trip, and they'd make it back to the cabin unscathed.

****

Freezing air and a torrent of snowflakes covered them immediately and undid all the warming from the furnace in the barn. Sabastian pushed the door wider, and they looked into the snow-lit darkness. He turned to her. "This doesn't look good."

She shivered and shook her head, pulling her scarf tighter when it threatened to blow off her head. "No, it doesn't."

"Do we risk it?

"Your hesitation is telling," he said when she didn't respond, and he hurriedly pulled her back to push the door against the other. "There's no point in making the barn colder while we decide. Do you want to stay here with the horses tonight?"

She pulled her thick top lip in and held it between her teeth, as her eyes searched his. "I don't know. What if the blizzard lasts for days and we are truly stuck here? The horses will be fine for a few days at least. But we may not be too comfortable... On the other hand, what if we can't make it back to the house in that white downpour?"

He glanced back to the tractor. "How much do you trust it to get us back?"

She shivered. "A lot actually. But I'm more concerned about getting lost in the whiteout. I'm wondering if we should wait until daybreak and then give it a try."

"It's up to you. I'm good either way."

"I think it's a good idea to stay."

"Then I do too."

The relief on Sebastian's face settled it as far as Celestia was concerned. "Then we stay."

"I noticed blankets in the tack room. Let's gather those, and see what else we can do to hunker down for the night."

"All right... And we can eat what I brought from the house, and then..." Celestia bit her bottom lip as she felt her cheeks heat. "I guess try to sleep?"

Sebastian nodded, watching her in such a way that she felt awkward and wanted to look away. His eyes bespoke hunger, but self-denial as well, if she was reading him right, and not projecting her own feelings on his gaze. She forced herself to retain eye contact even though the bashful feelings swamping her barely allowed her to do so.

"I am hungry," he said hesitantly, "And wouldn't mind

lying down. It's been a long day."

Celestia reached out and touched the area where his temple had turned a dark purple. She allowed her gaze to linger on the wound until she found the courage to look into his eyes. "Does it hurt much?"

His eyes seemed haunted before they closed briefly. When they opened again, a slight self-depreciating grin teased his lips. "No."

"Thank you for staying awake while I slept earlier. I hated asking it of you."

His growing smile eased the stress she'd seen building within his features, and Celestia sighed. She was so out of her depth here. The mountain of snow falling she could handle. A knockout gorgeous male who looked almost as lost as she felt was something else altogether.

"I enjoyed reading your aunt's book. She's got quite an imagination."

Celestia had to keep from telling him most of what her aunt wrote as fiction were actually things that happened to the family since they'd first found Mystic Mountain and all those years before, as well as what was stored in millennia of diaries. Of course, she'd changed all their ancestors' names, and altered the stories she read from their diaries, and according to her, most importantly, gave each cursed Cavanaugh woman a happily-ever-after ending. But who outside of their world would believe such a thing? And on the off chance they did, it put the family at risk.

Celestia's thoughts turned to the disaster of discovery, which had happened to Dia when she'd first met Ryan Steward, and decided she couldn't ever take the chance of revealing just who and what her family members were. Her cousin was nearly murdered, and the entire family had come under frightening scrutiny. And the sad truth was, Sabastian would likely be out of her life just as soon as they were able to make contact with the outside world.

The realization was almost too depressing to anticipate. She really liked him. A lot. But....

"Celestia?"

Celestia pulled herself from the deep abyss she'd fallen into. Her long nap failed to undo the damage of too many consecutive hours without sleep. She was still tired to the bone! Off kilter...and in an odd situation where she was alone with a man who made her feel all kinds of strange things that made no sense.

She took a cleansing breath. "Um, yes, she has a big imagination from what my cousins have said. As I said this morning, I haven't really had an opportunity to read her books yet. But I hope to once I get my life set up."

They wandered together back to the tack room and Sabastian surprised her by taking her hand into his. She glanced at him as they stopped before the open door and couldn't help but smile. "What are you doing?"

"Testing the waters."

Her brows shot up. "I see."

His head tilted slightly. "Are we good?"

She nodded slowly, deciding she liked the feel of being physically connected to someone else after spending a lifetime trying to avoid such a thing. "We are."

"I want to kiss you again."

She wanted it too and decided to stop living her life with what-ifs. She had for too long. Forever really. With the exception of her sister Luna, the Cavanaugh descendants were a brave and uninhibited lot who traditionally grabbed life by the horns and then just held on for the ride. True, they sometimes ended up on their butts, but at least they had an adventure getting there. It was a little disheartening to realize she'd never had a real adventure of her own.

Celestia blew out a breath and spoke before she lost her nerve, "Then kiss me."

Sabastian's fingers were immediately beneath her scarf

and sliding into her hair at the scalp. His lips started out gentle, again, but this time he deepened the kiss, and everything inside her melted. She reached for him and grasped his biceps, needing the anchor. She was afraid she'd float to the ceiling otherwise. He continued tasting and tantalizing her mouth, fogging her brain, and she had no choice but to respond with a hunger she never knew she had. When he finally eased away, their breath came out in quick spurts of steamy air, making her realize just how much the temperature in the barn dropped because they had opened the doors.

Sabastian lowered his hands and stepped back. "You taste…."

The lost look in his eyes helped to ease her conflicting emotions. If he'd been cocky or self-assured, it would have killed the moment completely. "You too."

"The blankets…"

She nodded quickly, realizing he was changing the subject to ease the tension that had taken over the air "Yes. And the hayloft…we can make a soft clean bed up there. As the heat increases in here the higher we are, the warmer it will be."

"I don't want you to worry I'd…."

"I don't. I know. I trust you."

Surprise lit his eyes. "Are you sure?"

"Yes."

Who was this confident, excited woman speaking these words, Celestia wondered, somewhat fascinated. When had she ever wanted, no, *needed*, to be so close to another human being, a male at that? She'd never allowed much thought of being touched intimately—and with the way she felt right now—with the thrill of giving into a wild abandon that was so out of character. She'd always carried herself with dignity, with reserve. She'd been so busy setting her life up, brick by careful brick, but more than that were risks she'd feared testing. Just thinking such thoughts brought shivers.

There had always been hesitancy to dream when it came to finding love for her kin. Even over the past couple of decades, with the three-thousand-year-old love curse broken by her mother and aunts, each Cavanaugh descendant who did attempt love had to fight through some kind of crazy or scary issue just to be able to secure it. She hadn't wanted any part. She'd found flaws with every man who had attempted getting close to her. She had discouraged flirting and all efforts at courting. Until meeting Sabastian, it had been easy.

Even telling herself she didn't know him from Adam, even reminding herself he could belong to another, and even fearing she wasn't up to something crazy like her sister and her cousins had experienced in finding their mates, changed nothing.

She wanted him. And she wanted him badly.

Celestia refused to let the questions take hold any longer than it took to think them. She wanted him. She wanted this. And for once in her life, she was going to let go and take exactly what every other Cavanaugh woman in their long and disastrous family history took when the man they wanted showed up in their lives.

A chance at love. A chance for happiness. A chance that it wouldn't all turn out horribly wrong.

Chapter Seven

The woman was everything a man would want. Bright, intelligent, and beautiful beyond imagination. Sabastian didn't want to ruin the moment with practicalities, or logic. But he didn't want to mess up what might be the most meaningful relationship of his life.

The problem was he didn't know what that life had held or if a relationship was even in the works. He was pretty sure he wasn't married, and he doubted he could be in love with another when everything about Celestia drew him in. But there were other things. Like was he a good guy? And if so, why would someone have thrown him out of an airplane? Or, if not that, why had he been left to die naked and alone in the snowy woods?

He stepped from her, knowing he couldn't move forward with her. At least not yet. Not until he had some answers.

She deserved better than that.

"I'm tired."

Though she recovered quickly, the flash of confusion, and what he felt was disappointment, was there for that fleeting second. He couldn't leave it alone and walk away, even though he knew that would be the best thing for both of them. "It isn't that I don't want you. It's that I do."

A second, then two, ticked by, before she nodded. "I see."

"Do you? Really?"

A grin spread her lips wide. "You're a very nice guy."

"I hope so."

Celestia reached up and touched his jaw, and warmth

flowed through him.

"You doubt it?"

Sabastian knew there was no point in speculating, and he really was beginning to feel the effects of his ordeal since awakening on the mountain however many hours ago it had been. "I don't know... I should know who I am and how I got here, especially the way I got here. What if my memories suddenly return, and I really am a dangerous man? What if I'm a prison escapee? Or a serial killer? What if I have devious urges and the fact I am so seriously attracted to you puts you in danger?"

It was obvious his words startled her, as her eyes widened briefly. Sabastian cringed at the turn his mind had taken, especially since he had no idea where all that had come from. That she didn't respond immediately, but only looked at him as if she should exercise caution after all, made him feel like an idiot. "I don't know why I said all that."

Her expression eased as she searched his eyes. "You are confused, rightly so. But it's cold in here again, and I'm hungry and still tired too, so we'll table what-ifs for later. Besides, I don't believe you are any of those things. Even without your memories, I think your nature would still be there. And all I see is a very decent man I plan to spend time with for the next little while."

Sabastian expelled a rattled breath, hoping she was right. Having said the words, he couldn't extinguish them as nothing. There was a reason he was in the predicament he was in, and there was nothing good he could think of to make sense of it. The only positive outcome of his predicament was being stranded with this warmhearted, beautiful woman. He moved toward the ladder leading up to the loft with the blankets he quickly snagged from the tack room, relieved she at least thought him a good man, promising himself if he hadn't been one before, he would be one now. Which meant he had to keep his mind and his hands to himself.

"Sabastian?"

He stopped with his foot on bottom rung and glanced back. "Yes?"

"I hope you don't mind, but could we snuggle at least? I'm chilled to the bone." When he stared at her and said nothing, her gaze fell to the floor. "Sharing body heat makes good sense. Don't you think?"

He nodded slowly, thinking the night was likely to be as long as the day had been. But she was right. They'd probably not freeze to death wrapped separately in blankets in the somewhat heated barn, but they'd both be much warmer together. He expelled a steamy breath. "Of course."

He was an idiot. There was no doubt about it. Just the thought of having her so close, of wrapping her against him to build and harness the warmth they would not otherwise gain, was practical on every level. He was just afraid the warmth he already felt at the image of her in his arms wasn't so pure of intent.

He forced those thoughts away and climbed the stacks of straw that would become their shelter for the night. After arranging the bales, he spread two of the blankets for them to lie upon before running his hands over the surface to assure their comfort. It took only light pounding to eliminate the occasional straw-end that threatened to poke at them throughout the night, and he was satisfied they were set.

Celestia appeared at his side with more blankets and the backpack. "I figured we might need them all."

He nodded and took them from her, placing three blankets on the makeshift bed, and rolling one to make them a shared pillow. The backpack he set on top.

"Good thinking."

He glanced back at Celestia to find her watching him with a caution he'd yet to see coming from her gaze. Her hesitancy to join him actually eased him, and he smiled and held out his hand. "You have nothing to fear from me," he said, relieved he believed the words himself.

Celestia grinned, a playful sparkle lighting her eyes. She jumped forward onto the bedding, making him laugh, until he heard the gasp and saw her jerking her hand back. She turned over and quickly placed a finger in her mouth as her eyes widened in fear.

Sabastian reacted swiftly, but forced himself to calm before grasping and gently removing her finger from her full lips. He looked down to find a large splinter had speared her delicate skin. The thing that took his breath was it looked like liquid silver seeped from her wound.

The loft expanded and contracted with dizzying speed. The pain of a sledgehammer against bone slammed into his chest. And his eardrums burst with what sounded like a sonic boom. Sabastian's body thrust back, banging his head on one of the crossbeams supporting the structure. His heart pounded, his head swam and his mind could grasp onto nothing, until finally, he felt Celestia's hand on his cheek. He focused just enough to see the concern in her eyes as she leaned over him.

"What happened? Are you okay? Sabastian! Are you okay?"

The panic in her voice pulled him back by increments. Sabastian? No. He wasn't Sabastian. He was Sabian. Former reaper of the dead. He was an angel. A heavenly being. Trapped in a human male's body. He was here on a mission. He was here to retrieve a soul lost, to procure the one with the silver blood, and to get his position back....

Sabian stared up at Celestia, absorbing her beauty, her kindness, her sweet spirit. Everything within him shuddered and cringed. Of all the things he was here to do, the most important was touching him with gentleness and staring straight into his eyes. He was here to deliver her into the hands of another. To take the life she knew and exchange it for something she could never fathom. Forever. For eternity.

He didn't have a chance to voice denial. Her lips were suddenly there, tasting him, teasing his mouth with the tentative touch of her tongue. His mind protested again, but this time it was from her touch. He couldn't make himself push her away. She tasted of the morning mist. She radiated warmth. And her scent was his undoing.

He grasped her on both sides of her face and pulled her in deeper, taking her mouth on the exotic dance of lovers. Sabian reveled in the moment, allowing his hands to slide through her long white tresses, down her firm but tiny shoulders, and then inward until he felt the rapidly rising and falling of her thickly covered breasts. The desire to see her bared, to touch the soft fullness of her breasts, caused his hips to jerk of their own accord and his already swollen penis to tighten even more. He fumbled with the zipper of her parka, certain he'd break the zipper if it didn't comply quickly. Once the thick garment opened, his hands went on a mission of discovery, but cupping the large still material encased globes didn't satisfy him. He tugged her shirt upward, and slid his hands beneath her bra.

He broke the kiss to look at her beautiful breasts, to capture their soft weight, to stroke the hard dark nipples as her head fell back and a moan escaped her lips. He leaned forward, unable to deny the desperate need to taste, and clasped one nipple between his teeth. She jerked in reaction, curling forward, but he couldn't stop. Overwhelming desire to strip her naked wracked his body making his mouth less adoring and more aggressive. A small voice said to stop, to ease up, to make sure he wasn't hurting her, but he only growled as he continued to suckle and nip at the nipple that seemed to have become his lifeline.

Time stretched and yawned before anything penetrated the insatiable hunger ravaging his mind. Eventually a smidgen of sanity returned, allowing him awareness her hands were at his chest, pulling at his jacket. He wanted to help her but only ended up thwarting her efforts to fulfill the desperate raging craving to get her naked as quickly as possible. While he tugged at her clothing, and she struggled to do the same with his, he nipped and licked her flesh, ravishing every inch of her he could reach. Once her shirt and bra had gone the way of her parka, he struggled out of his own clothing from the waist up, with every intention of stripping them the rest of the way once he could stand to release his hold.

She seemed as frantically in need as he, which only intensified his own desire. She lowered her head and their lips converged and caught hold, as if magnets with opposing pull. He felt her hands slide over his torso with as frantic a pace as his were over her. He wanted to feel every inch of her. To know every curve and crevice. To taste all he was touching. He pulled back only for oxygen then dove for her lips again, and their tongues wrestled with less grace and more hunger. He'd never experienced anything so explosive, so all encompassing, as kissing her made him feel. She radiated happiness, excitement, and the rapid beat of his human heart somehow filled him with an energy that surpassed the only other thing in his existence that had fulfilled him...doing the job he'd been created to perform.

The reminder was like a slap in the face, and he jerked back, banging his head against the barn's siding again.

Celestia's large eyes were clearly startled, and he knew it was because she'd been as caught up in the moment as he. He cleared his throat, unsure of how to defuse the pulsing that still held his body in such a tight grip, and wondered how his straining penis didn't burst the skin surrounding it. He swallowed and reached out to her with shaking hands.

"We have to stop."

She pulled back quickly, and her lost look nearly made him throw caution to the sky. But he couldn't. Not only would he lose what had started in his human heart to feel like he imagined love would feel, he'd lose his very existence. When Celestia said nothing but continued to stare at him, Sabian exhaled loudly and allowed his hands to fall to his sides. With another deep breath, he began what he knew would be a long line of lies.

There was no way he could tell her why he was here. The woman was pure. Innocent. She would have to remain that way if he were to fulfill his mission, satisfy The Creator, and sustain an existence once everything was done to the Master's satisfaction.

Celestia shuffled her weight to the side with her head lowered and her long white bangs hiding her eyes. Without looking up, she crossed one arm over her chest to cover herself and moved from atop his legs to settle at his side. She still faced him, but the rigidness of her hunched pose made it clear she was not only confused but embarrassed as well. Sabian knew what it was to experience regret. He wanted to tell her why he'd suddenly stopped, why he couldn't let what was about to happen ever happen, when it was so clear they'd both been equally captivated by the other. But he couldn't. Not now. Not yet.

At least not honestly.

Until he fulfilled his first mission, to take the earthly life of the woman who had escaped death once already, he couldn't even show her that he was what he was. Even with his memories returned, without his celestial powers, he was still nothing more than a human male. One who, by human standards, was about to find someone he didn't know just to murder her. Then without delay, kidnap the woman he was afraid had quickly and thoroughly stolen his heart.

****

"What did I do wrong?"

She forced herself to lift her head and look him in the eyes. The sadness she saw in his eased her hurt somewhat.

A flash of confusion widened his eyes for only seconds before he shook his head.

"You did nothing wrong."

She stared at him with doubt, but the sincerity of his words finally penetrated. "Then what? While you were devouring me you suddenly remembered a wife?"

A hint of amusement tilted his lips but he shook his head. "No. Only a vow of celibacy."

Celestia was certain her already pale skin turned whiter. "Are you saying you're a priest?"

He hesitated, and she could tell he was struggling with his answer. She waited and hurt turned to anger. Although she'd be lying to say none was directed at him, the reality was her building fury had more to do with fate. Of all the men she could have felt the *claiming* bond with, the only one who appealed to her senses was married to God! She shook her head in dismay. It wasn't fair! Her cousins and sister had found the ones they were destined to claim. Obstacles were always there but were manageable... eventually. This was not. Not only did her family believe in the highest of powers, they'd all been instilled with the knowledge it was only by His grace they were who and what they were. She reached out to Sabastian's thankfully still covered calves to claim her shirt, quickly pulling it on. She didn't have the patience, or steady enough hands, to handle the hooks and eyes of a bra.

"I'm sorry," Sabastian said softly.

Celestia couldn't look at him or respond. She was mortified and felt her body withering from within as she moved back and climbed into their makeshift bed. She pushed the backpack out of the way, toward him, no longer hungry herself. She turned to face the wall, hoping he would take the hint and leave her in whatever peace she could find.

She'd been a good girl all her life. Never stepped out of others' established bounds. Never been in trouble even for the smallest offence. Of her two siblings and six cousins, who were all the same age, she was the one everyone believed had it all together. They'd assumed her unmoved by the disappointing results following the ceremony that should have given her a magical gift, because she'd refused to let them believe differently.

But she was a fraud. She'd kept hope alive all these years. She was a Cavanaugh as much as she was a Hansen. And Cavanaughs held magic. She'd never let herself consider her life would be nothing more than hard study and the work she loved. Outside of caring for animals, her life was bland, as colorless as her hair. Looking within now, she had to acknowledge how shamefully envious she'd been when the others learned of their gifts, even when attaining those gifts had nearly cost each one's life. Of the nine of them, only she and Soleli were still waiting... and, as time kept moving on, she feared there were none left for either of them to claim. And maybe that went for finding their own lovers as well.

As her mother had said many times—perhaps fearful her daughters wouldn't wield any—magic always came with a high price. But Celestia hadn't cared, and she suspected her sisters hadn't either. She'd desperately wanted it for herself all this time, especially now, since she knew she couldn't claim the man her body and soul yearned for. It was so little to ask that she get what all Cavanaugh women expected. So reasonable to hope for. So unfair when others had what she so desperately wanted. Most didn't make a habit of using what they'd been given… as if it meant little or nothing.

Her youngest sister, Luna, now a mermaid when within Mystic Lake's waters, was able to heal both earth and bodies while in the lake's magical depths. But other than changing to human form on land, and mermaid when in the lake, Celestia didn't know if Luna ever used her healing powers now the lake was once again restored. Their cousin Sapphire was able to shape shift on land and perform magic with a wave of her hand, though she had hardly ever used her gifts and made it clear she would not unless absolutely necessary. Sapphire's youngest sister, Diamond, as Ryan had surely told her by now, was able to destroy or replenish the earth and control all natural elements if she so chose. But her memories had been taken at her own request, so she hadn't even had a chance to practice her power. Their sister Jewell was able to transport through time and take on the life of another, but she chose to be nothing more than a stay-at-home mom, now that she had children. And her male cousins were no better. Zeus, Apollo and Heracles had all gotten the ability to perform magic immediately following the Ascension Ceremony when they'd all turned fifteen. Celestia couldn't remember the last time the brothers used magic at all.

Refusing to think about the movements Sabastian was making behind her, Celestia concentrated on her family history and its constant disappointments. According to the recorded diaries of those who came before the curse was broken by her mother and aunts, it was a given each with Cavanaugh blood had to ascend to obtain the full measure of their gift, which began to manifest in their thirteenth year. As all Cavanaughs were, she been taught, at midnight the day they turned fifteen, a sacrifice had to be made with the *Blood of Continuation* to attain ascension and solidify the mystical gift bestowed.

But nothing had been the same once the curse was broken.

For her generation, not only did the gifts come haphazardly, and at odd times in each individual's life—if they came at all—there were now males born to Cavanaugh women for the first time in over three thousand years. And the most astounding change was more than one of the triplets was capable of procreating. Over three millennia, only the single chosen Cavanaugh woman in each generation had born offspring to carry on the line. Then the chosen one's identical sisters became caretakers and teachers of the fruitful sister's children. That her mother, and both sisters, had not only gotten to keep the loves of their lives, all three had been able to bear children. But then... they were the destined chosen identified in the curse all those years ago.

The Three.

As a result, Celestia and her cousins were all born on the same day, within minutes of each other. Two sets of triplet girls, and a set of triplet boys. They'd all grown up with many best friends, and though they'd made more after entering public school, no one outside of the family was allowed to get too close. Sleepovers and friend parties were allowed, but only once their parents knew the other kids' parents, and never at a Cavanaugh descendant's house. With all the magical things that regularly happened, it was too dangerous to allow outsiders in.

And that had been fine. Not a problem in the least. They'd all grown up knowing the most important thing about being a Cavanaugh was to protect themselves and the family from exposure and possible investigation. People wouldn't understand, and what they didn't understand, they feared. Fear would lead to anger and actions that historically had sent Cavanaughs of generations before fleeing for their lives—or dead.

None of that mattered to Celestia. All she wanted was to have a magical ability she and others would have a need to protect. All she needed was to know the blood of her ancestors flowed in her veins as well. And all she desired was to know the kind of love her mother and father shared.

"Celestia?"

She cringed as she huddled deeper into the covers.

"I'm sorry. I shouldn't have let things go as far as they did."

Like a switch being flipped, hurt and embarrassment turned to anger. She rolled over and looked up where he'd settled at her feet. "Don't! I don't want to talk about this. I just want to go to sleep."

Sabastian nodded slowly. "I understand. Would you prefer I went down and made a bed for myself elsewhere?"

As quickly as her anger had flared, it dissipated. He looked exhausted, and if she was reading the regret in his eyes right, hurt as well. Damn! She didn't want to feel sorry for him when she was doing such a stellar job of feeling sorry for herself. Celestia blew out a breath, letting it take the tension from her neck and shoulders. "No. Of course not. Come on. Let's both try to get some sleep."

****

Sabian listened to Celestia's even breathing as he stared at the slant of the roof and level rafters above his head, wondering what he was to do next. His mind was mush. His human body had weakening significantly. But still, he couldn't shut down and rest.

Three hours had passed since they'd said goodnight. He'd pretended to sleep for a while, just as she had. Each keeping from touching the other. He was relieved when, about thirty or so minutes in, her body relaxed and her breathing became less stifled and more measured. But it wasn't until he'd felt her unintentionally align her body against his in the tight quarters of their makeshift bed that he knew she was truly out.

It should have made him relax... But just the opposite was true. Her innocent touch had instantly reignited the fires in his loins. He reached over and slid his hand between their touching hips, then followed the curve of hers with his fingers. He pulled his hand away quickly when she sighed and remained frozen until she settled back into the rhythmic breathing pattern again.

Sabian closed his eyes and let his mind wander. He went over the missions assigned, the consequences of not achieving the goals set for him. He was in way over his head. Without his angelic supremacies, he had nothing with which to accomplish his goals in a neat and clean fashion. What was once a simple matter of thinking of where he wanted to be, and then being there, was now the complicated act of accepting kindness from others to take him where he needed to go. Which took away any possibility of privacy. The ability to achieve these goals with a flick of thought was now going to be dependent on him physically performing acts humans would deem criminally abhorrent. And sinful.

Though he'd never felt a second's guilt in collecting souls, taking an actual life filled Sabian's midsection with a squirming, ill feeling. Worse, after having received such wonderful care from the woman who had saved his life and seeing to what lengths Celestia was willing to go to get him to safety, he knew there was no way she'd understand his mission, even if he was allowed to reveal it. Which he wasn't. All he could hope was she had no knowledge of the woman he had to find, stalk, and kill when the opportunity presented itself.

Sabian had to take measured breaths just to get through this last thought.

Shivers tingled over every inch of his human body, and chill-bumps blanketed the skin covering it. He hadn't bargained on feeling merciless about any of this when this mission was laid-out, but he'd only had moments to process what was being required of him. All he'd been concerned about was getting his purpose in existing back, and seeing the dawn of many a new earthly day.

Being created for the sole purpose of Soul Reaper was a high honor in the Angelic Realm. Especially prestigious when one was able to deliver a soul to the Heavenly Host—and even though far less desirable for all, when transporting those souls who never would enter The Heavenly Gates.

Taking the damned to their destination was definitely less appealing but still heralded a worthy purpose for a Reaper's existence. After all, that task, too, was required once *mind-capable creation* refused to accept The Creator as such during their lifespan.

He'd loved his existence. He'd enjoyed his purpose. He'd learned so much about all the species of the earth and how they had changed, or been eliminated, over time. He'd seen man create amazing things with the brain The Creator gave them. And he'd seen unimaginable evil done by those whose souls they'd sold for thirty pieces of silver, give or take.

He'd witnessed the first sin and subsequent fall of all mankind that followed. He'd been unimaginably busy following the flood of human souls needing transport to eternal damnation after the earth and sky covered the planet with water. He'd been mesmerized at times by the human spirit and imagination; from the woman who first discovered a way to make fire without lightning, through the years of tool building to assist in improving what humans considered their lot in life, to navigating beyond where they'd believed the earth ended at the horizon. He'd laughed at some attempts humans fumbled their way through, and then would shake his head in wonder when they managed to build large cities or incredible pyramids with nothing more than determination, blood, sweat and tears. And he'd been truly impressed when they devised a way to take themselves off the planet to survive in the heavens within small metal cones.

Time over time, each step forward resulted in many steps back, but once seduced by the sin of the serpent, humans reprogrammed to reach for that which was just beyond their touch. In that was sin, yes, since all should find peace and contentment with what The Creator allotted. But Sabian had silently admired that trait in the final creations, as he too had always wanted more than was his to have. He still did.

He wanted Celestia as his own. He craved her as a human male, but knowing she was destined for, and capable of surviving in, the Angelic Realm, he knew too she could partner him throughout eternity... if he was given back eternity.

Until meeting her, he'd never given thought to having a partner, a companion, or knowing the touch of a loving hand. Now he craved it to the marrow of the bones this human body held. Only he had to let such thoughts go. It mattered not that he'd been given these feelings to experience. They were no doubt another form of punishment for his own sins. And of course, a test of his obedience.

Sabian exhaled a weary breath, knowing he would never have an eternity if he did not fulfill his duties as laid out. He couldn't have Celestia. He would disappear as if he had never been if he defied this demand, defiled her purity so she could not fulfil her own purpose within the ranks of the Brotherhood.

He had to stop thinking about it and let any such thoughts fill him with fear rather than desire. But as the night moved on without sleep, all he could think of was turning to her and taking her into passions embrace.

Chapter Eight

Some things would always be just inches beyond full understanding... Like awakening suddenly, yet still being on that uneven plane of Neverland where one couldn't quite grasp what was happening. Until the mind cleared, or thought it did, and realized that weird sound and the flashing white light was a cell phone's alarm going off... although certain it was never set to go wild at four forty-five on a Friday morning to begin with.

Rattled, and knowing her cell phone was dead and couldn't be the culprit, Celestia remained very still, knowing—but not knowing why—she should. It took several heart-racing seconds for her to fully accept it wasn't an alarm that pulled her from a slumber so deep she remembered nothing but the blackness of it, but instead was possibly from the dream she was certain she'd had in spite of evidence to the contrary.

Something about the eerily quiet barn *felt* wrong.

Celestia cautiously glanced to her side where Sabastian made no sounds. The horses were likewise silent, giving her a sensation of abandonment. Even the wind, which had whistled around the barn earlier, must have died down to lie as dormant as the world the snow covered. She turned her head slowly again, as her sight adjusted to changing degrees of darkness in the barn's loft. She was grateful she'd left the single light on in the tack room below, though it did little to help but make unusual shadows on the higher ceiling beyond the upper floor.

Her breath caught when she detected a shift in the shadows. Chilling seconds after detecting another's presence, she recognized the curvaceous outline of her cousin's exquisite nude shape. Celestia simultaneously exhaled in relief and shoved down her aggravation. Sapphire had nearly frightened her to death.

Her more shadowed than illuminated cousin lifted a finger to her pursed lips then tilted her head to the side. Celestia nodded and slowly slid out of the covers, careful not to touch the man next to her. She was still too befuddled to deduce what day it was or the time, but now that a member of her family had finally made it to her, she knew the little reprieve she'd taken from her everyday life was over.

Which was just as well.

Just the scent of the man sleeping so soundly at her side made her want to forget he was a priest. That he had pledged his life to God and the church. She wanted to let loose in a way she'd never before imagined and find out what it felt like to know him intimately. Were it not for the history of the women in her family regarding such things, she would have been seriously concerned about her sanity in so desperately desiring a man she barely knew. The *claiming* instinct was beyond their control, once the one they were supposed to claim popped into their lives.

As she made to way to where Sapphire stood majestically, she marveled at her cousin's ability to dress herself fully with a single wave of her hand. Celestia felt not only envy at her cousin's ability to wield magic with such assurance, but an inkling of resentment reared its head that she herself had no such ability to change those things that did not suit her. Like her present predicament.

They went quietly down the ladder, though Celestia knew Sapphire took the steps in deference to Celestia's inability to jump or transport as her cousin could. She passed Sapphire at the landing to peek in at both Cleo and Cleopatra to find both standing with their heads down, and eyes closed.

"I gave them a little extra push to keep them from waking when I entered. I didn't want to frighten them. Or you."

Celestia turned back and nodded. "Thank you."

Knowing Sapphire followed her, Celestia walked to the far end of the barn silently. She was dying to know what was going on with the family and to talk to someone who would understand what was happening in her own life. From the first moment Sapphire laid eyes on Nicolae, the Lycanthrope Alpha, she'd told the family of a connection that had been both the beginning and the end for her. She hadn't been able to break the magical, though invisible bonds tying them together, and hadn't had any desire to, at least not until he'd done the unthinkable. But they'd worked through it, and she'd claimed him, as was the way of the women of the Cavanaugh Clan.

Only Celestia couldn't do the same. Not now. Not ever. As much power as her family possessed, as much strength as the men and even the women in their coven bore as both blessing and curse, there were still taboos no one dared cross.

And taking a servant of God from His services, to use for their own purposes, was the big one.

"Who is that gorgeous man?"

"He's a priest."

Sapphire's perfectly arched black eyebrows shot up. "Seriously?"

Not able to contain a grin at her cousin's reaction, Celestia nodded.

"Well, that explains why I didn't find you both naked and wrapped around each other. How did he come to be here?"

Celestia swallowed, relieved her cousin hadn't arrived when they had indeed been half-naked and wrapped together as close as they could get at the time. Her ability to see as well in the dark as in daylight would have left nothing to the imagination. "We believe he may have fallen out of an airplane."

Sapphire said nothing, nor did she move. Finally, she took a deep breath and exhaled. "Why would you both believe that? Does he not know?"

Shaking her head, Celestia shrugged. "He was naked and nearly dead when I found him. I think only Cleopatra's warmth kept him alive. She was with him. I was on Cleo hunting for her in the snowstorm. He doesn't know why he was naked or why he was here. He didn't remember anything about himself until he suddenly was certain he was a priest."

"How would he be certain of only that if he remembers nothing else? Did something jog his memory?"

Celestia swallowed and nodded, knowing her face was too heated not to give her away. "We were about to... You know."

Amusement lit Sapphires blue eyes, transforming them to the bright yellow that indicated the wolf in her was awakening. Celestia had only seen her cousin transform into her wolf-form a handful of times. She knew she had no reason to fear it happening now, yet she couldn't stop herself from taking a step back. Over a span of a few seconds, Sapphire's irises settled back to their normal sapphire blue, and Celestia relaxed.

"You never need fear me," she said, a hint of hurt in her tone.

"I know. It was instinctual, not deliberate. Please forgive me. But why did you react in this way?"

A slow grin curled Sapphire's lips. "Because I am in estrus, and the thought of you and him together, or any mating for that matter, brings out the beast in me. I fear Nicolae is in for a wild ride for the next few days. In both forms."

Celestia was happy to see her cousin so excited at the prospect of trying to conceive again. She'd done so early in her and Nicolae's relationship, but for reason she hadn't shared to Celestia's knowledge, she'd miscarried before anyone knew how many children were lost. For weeks after the loss Sapphire's normally outgoing, take-charge spirit had dimmed. Silent and withdrawn, she'd not talked about the loss, nor had the family pushed her to speak of it once she'd told them there would be no reason to have the baby shower her mother was in the process of planning. Celestia moved forward and wrapped Sapphire in her arms before stepping back. "I am so happy for you."

The light in Sapphire's eyes dimmed slightly. "I haven't told anyone else yet that we are going to try again, so please don't say anything. I'm afraid. What if it happens again? What if the rabies I was infected with or the changes my body went through to make me Lycanthrope won't allow me to carry children?

"It broke my heart into tiny pieces the last time, but worse, it took something deep from within Nicolae. He's still the man I cherish, and he treats me like gold, but with his past, the loss hit him even harder than me."

Celestia nodded, knowing her cousin-in-law had lost his parents at a young age, in a way that would have taken the spirit of a lesser man. That he recovered what amounted to the ultimate betrayal, able to forgive those who had brought harm, said so much about his character. Of all the men her cousins had found and fallen in love with, Celestial felt a special affection for the man who made this cousin so happy.

She grasped Sapphire's hand and looked deeply into her eyes. "We won't believe those things possible. You have a heart meant for mothering, and I know in my own heart, you will have the family you both desire."

Serenity replaced the fear in those sapphire eyes as she squeezed Celestia's hand. "There is a peace that flows from you, and I believe your words hold truth."

Sapphire's statement was startling…confusing, even. Celestia felt the peace of their physical connection as well. It was odd, this low humming throughout her body, and the certainty she was making a declaration of truth, not just offering platitudes. She sent her cousin a shaky smile, hoping they were both right, yet afraid to trust what might be a desperation to matter on a deeper level to their mystical family. Was it possible she'd finally found her Gift? Was it possible she had the power of knowledge?

Excitement danced though her, and Celestia closed her eyes as she shivered in delight. She couldn't deny it to herself any longer now that it seemed possible she had found her gift. She really had given up hope. She'd feared neither she nor her sisters would be gifted like past generations, and her cousins in this one. Until it happened for her baby sister. And even then, she'd not trusted it would happen for her or Soleli.

There was always an Enchantress, capable of casting or conjuring. A Regulator, who controlled natural elements. And The Divine whose spirit was free to discover truth. Though for each individual, the gift manifested in a distinctly different way. Luna had already received her gift as Regulator with the additional ability to heal within the lake waters. It was still possible for Soleli and herself to have one of the other two and whatever special ability manifested for each of them.

"Celestia?"

Celestia shook the thought away, knowing she could possibly just be grasping at straws. Just because the words she'd spoken to Sapphire felt like absolute truth didn't mean they were true. Nor did it mean she had found her gift. But it was something to think about and investigate. If she was wrong the entire family would pity her, and that she couldn't abide. Worse, they'd feel bad themselves they had what she also desperately wanted. And there was no way she would do that to any of them. She wouldn't share this terrifying excitement with anyone yet.

"Celestia, are you okay?"

Huffing out a little laugh, Celestia backed away and purposefully sent a gaze to the loft. "I don't want to awaken him yet. Let's step outside."

Sapphire nodded slowly, frowning with curiosity, making Celestia wonder just how long she'd been lost in thought, or if anxiety was written all over her face.

Having never been so rattled, Celestia took deep even breaths and turned with what she hoped was a sincere smile. "Never mind. I'll wait until he is awake, and we'll go back to the cabin. What are your plans?"

Sapphire shrugged. "There still seems to be a problem contacting everyone, so I'm going to continue on up the mountain and check on Dia. I hope Ryan was with her through all this."

Celestia's smile felt more natural at the thought of Dia and Ryan. While opening the barn door only wide enough to allow them to exit, she quickly told Sapphire of enlightening Dia of the past. She was rewarded with amusement in the dark beauty's eyes.

"I'll approach their cabin loudly then, so I don't catch them in a compromising position!"

She and Sapphire laughed together before her cousin transformed into the little wolf and took off at a run across the snow-covered field and into the trees in the distance. The freedom to fly, if only over the mountainous terrain, sent a tug of envy into Celestia's chest. She felt so earthbound. So stuck in place. Not only physically, but emotionally as well.

Celestia turned and reentered the barn, closing the

door behind her. Her breath hung in the air, and she knew she'd allowed too much cold in while parting with Sapphire. Hurrying across the barn, she couldn't help but smile when both Cleo and Cleopatra's heads suddenly appeared above the half doors of their stalls. She went to one then the other, offering them greetings and affection.

"Good morning."

Celestia turned swiftly to find Sabastian making his way down the ladder. He stopped at the bottom and held onto the fifth rung as he sent her what she could only call a cautious smile. She knew her own was as stilted, and the irritation of the night before returned. "Good morning."

Sabastian moved toward her, hesitated, then bypassed Cleo to head straight to Cleopatra. The mare whinnied in delight, and Cleo snorted before pulling his teeth back in a sneer. Celestia shook her head at the large stallion, and he settled immediately.

"You need to make friends with him as well."

Sabastian slid Cleo a glance before turning his attention on Celestia. "He wants to bite me."

Surprise lifted her brows. Not because she doubted it, but because Sabastian knew it as well. "How do you know that?"

Sabastian shrugged and lifted his hand to Cleopatra's jaw to stroke it when she nudged him. "When I stepped down he looked at me from behind your back, and those eyes held dire warning."

"You are very perceptive. I feel his anger at you as well. Still, perhaps you just need to make the effort."

Sabastian hesitated, and then nodded. "I'll do that, if you will make sure he doesn't kill me."

Celestia laughed. "You believe I can control all that muscle?" She sobered. "Seriously, though, Cleo is a lover, not a fighter."

He nodded as though he had his doubts. "You have a

way with them. I think he would die to please you." His lips twisted. "And to keep me from touching his girlfriends."

Cleo's head went up and down sharply a few times, making Celestia's laughter natural. She moved to him, and reached up to scratch behind his pointed ears. "You are a good boy, my Cleo. Now be nice to Sabastian. He's not going to hurt me or Cleopatra."

****

Sabian had to keep from reacting to the hard pawing Cleo made against the stall's floor. The horse was smart and knew there was something about him that posed a threat to Celestia. Although he didn't believe the horse could possibly know Sabian was there to take Celestia from the life she now had, he sensed something. The horse needed to be watched closely and handled with care. Having a human body, feeling aggravating pain and wielding no angelic supremacies, put him at a great disadvantage if the horse decided to trample him to death. He moved closer, hoping Celestia's calming hand on the horse saved his sorry butt.

Cleo watched him with a sharp gaze that never eased, though he allowed Sabian to touch his jaw. But only for a second. The large head jerked up, and Sabian took a quick step back before sending Celestia a look, making his point.

She frowned and shook her head. "I don't understand this. Cleo is such a sweet guy."

Sabian understood it completely, but he was in no position to enlighten her. Of all of the animals in creation, the horse held a special place with The Creator. Not only was the most efficient and beautiful of forms their gift, they also held knowledge humans would never know of or understand. Their ability to see beyond what was right in front of them and the ability to process thought beyond their own survival had carried them through the ages. It also made them suffer deep emotional distress when not rightly cared for. Instead of revealing Cleo's abilities, Sabian shrugged away her comment. "Like I said, he doesn't like me."

When she turned to kiss the long nose and offer a softly spoken admonishment to the stallion, Sabian exhaled a long breath. He was ready to get away from the barn and hoped they could get to safer ground as soon as possible. If Celestia had as deep an affinity with the animal as it seemed, she might start mistrusting Sabian too. And that he couldn't afford.

She headed past him to the large doors of the barn and slid them open, revealing a bright white world where the snow no longer fell. The visual purity was a swift reminder of the world he wanted to reenter in the higher heavens, and he used the thoughts building to propel him into action and purpose. With his memories restored, he was obligated to begin his duties. Which meant he had to close down the feelings his human brain allowed and become, once again, a vessel with only one mission. To secure his charges, and to deliver them to their eternal stations.

"We should be able to make our way back to my parents' cabin. The snow will have settled by now, and though it's deep, the tractor should make it easy enough. Do you want to hop on and start it? I'll take care of the doors."

Sabian nodded and jumped aboard the large conveyor, glad he hadn't had to make the suggestion. He started the tractor with efficient movements, now he knew what to do, and backed out slowly. The transition from the solid floor to the shelf of snow at the entrance wasn't any more difficult than a small slip and slight lifting of the large rear tires as they conquered the conversion. Outside in the chilly air, which cleared the lingering fog from his mind, Sabian allowed the crispness to fill his lungs and send vapors with each exhaled breath, even though the difference of breathing the colder air hurt his chest a little. Just as the upcoming changes about to affect Celestia would hurt her.

Though she didn't know it, today was the beginning of their end. Ignoring the jab of regret, Sabian said nothing as he waited for her to secure the barn and climb aboard at this side. He tried not to let her big smile as she took his hand to step up affect him, nor the light of pleasure in her beautiful eyes as she settled. He silently swore he wasn't affected by the sweet scent of hay clinging to her. Nor, he vowed, did her slight form bring out protective instincts in the male body he'd been burdened with. As he threw the tractor into gear once more, he focused on the task of returning them to the warmth of the cabin and allowed his thoughts to go no further.

Chapter Nine

"We should attempt getting to town."

Though she felt her words a little clipped, Celestia didn't know how else to get them moving now that they'd made it back to her parents' cabin.

Clearing on the winding mountain road would be a priority by the state's Department of Transportation. She could give over the care of this amnesiac priest to the local Catholic Church and then get to her clinic. They both could get on with their separate lives. He'd barely said a word to her since they'd returned to the cabin. She'd hardly known what to say either, which had left them both glancing at each other with awkward expressions too many times for her to count. That Sabastian merely nodded was the final straw.

"You could at least say something!"

Sabastian stopped in the process of pulling on the parka he'd worn to the barn, and looked her way. "Thank you for all that you've done."

The starch went out of shoulders Celestia didn't even know were stiff. "You don't need to thank me. I was happy to help."

He searched her face making heat rush to her cheeks.

"I'm sorry things got out of hand. I hope we can be friends."

There was hateful laughter locked within her throat, but Celestia refused to allow it to pass her lips. It wasn't his fault they were in these positions, but for some reason that didn't ease the angst she felt toward him. "Sure."

"You're angry. Why?"

How could she explain what made no sense to anyone outside of her wacky family? "I'm not angry."

"Yes, you are."

Celestia sent him an exasperated glare. "You're a priest. Don't they teach you guys to be too polite to say such things?"

Sabastian smiled, and for a second she was certain there was a hint of evil in it. That she would think such a thing of a godly man just went to prove how despicable her mind was at the moment. It wasn't like her and didn't sit well. She turned away and made herself busy putting her jacket on, only to feel his arms come around her from behind as his breath shifted the hairs over her ears.

"I know. I feel it too."

Celestia relaxed back against him. "You do?" She felt movement she interpreted as his nod.

"I do. I'm attracted to you…more than attracted. But I can't act on it."

There was satisfaction in his admission, along with irritation. She turned in his arms and looked up into his eyes. "Are you certain you're a priest?"

Something played across his eyes, and she knew he was debating with himself. It wasn't fair of her to ask such a question. "I'm sorry. Of course you are." She took a step back and he allowed her to go. After blowing out an uneven breath, she shook her head. "I think it best if I take you to town and hand you over to the parish. Then we can't see each other, ever again."

Panic flashed across his features before he advanced on her. He stopped inches in front of her, his eyes desperately searching hers.

"We have to! I need you to…."

He looked from left to right, and then closed his eyes tightly. When he opened them, he looked resigned.

"I'm not sure. I don't think I can have these feelings

for you, if I were a priest. Maybe I'm wrong. I don't remember anything else about myself, so maybe my fear of not knowing is what stopped me last night. I can say with all honesty I want to get to know you. I want to explore what is between us. But…."

Something akin to joy filled her, and Celestia couldn't help the smile that stretched the muscles of her cheeks. "I want to get to know you too, but if it can lead nowhere…."

"Let's get to town, and let me have a look around. Maybe something will click. Perhaps I just need to see something familiar and my memories will resurface."

Her nod was jerky, as was the breath leaving her lungs since excitement had once again taken hold. She knew she was grasping, wishing upon stars, but there was little she could do to avoid seizing hope, minimal though it was. If he could just remember and find he was free to explore their attraction, then everything else could work out. He seemed so open, so honest and completely without guile. It would take someone like that to accept her and her family. And the more she thought about it, the more certain she became. He was the one meant to be hers all along.

Celestia stepped away from him, still needing to guard her heart, although she knew it already lost. He didn't comment as they finished readying themselves, until it was time to walk back into the crisp air.

"If I am a priest, then I may have to rethink my calling."

His words were what her heart wanted to hear, but tentacles of fear reached out to encircle her. She mentally brushed them away, and then realized she made motions with her hands to do the same to her arms. That she'd visualized the glistening cords tipped with buds of light coming at her, stole her breath for seconds. Forcefully pulling herself together, she glanced back and was relieved to see Sabastian busy tying the shoelaces of her father's boots. He hadn't witnessed her odd moment. But again, it was something she'd have to file away to think on later.

With so many strange feelings, and now this burst of sight, she was almost certain her mystical gift was manifesting… *Finally*. But if that were so, what was it exactly? And why now?

"I need my mother."

Sabastian rose and tilted his head. "You said she was out of town."

Having not meant to say the words aloud, Celestia nodded, knowing to a normal person that would be a problem. But once she could get to a phone that worked, and get her mother on the problems she was experiencing, there would be nothing on earth capable of stopping her from helping in any way she could.

Little could be done if Sabastian did belong to the church, unless there was some out Celestia was unaware of. That aside, she needed help understanding these feelings and visions. If her mother didn't have any clues herself, she could consult the vast mountain of ancestral diaries to see if another Cavanaugh woman had the same symptoms and then see where her gifts led.

****

Sabian enjoyed the truck ride more than he'd expected. He'd always wondered why human males, mostly, got such a kick from traveling in such slow conveyances, but now it made sense. The hum of the powerful engine gave one the impression of inner strength. Though Celestia proceeded cautiously, it was still with more speed than humans could on their own power. The glass surrounding them gave a nearly unobstructed view of one new vista after another despite the limited change of scenery now. He looked forward to reaching town and getting a chance to look at and communicate with the human condition up close and personal.

The realization he'd have to play a role of deceit was settling in, though the slap of it was not as sharp as earlier. Lingering regret was something he knew he would have to overcome quickly, as well as finding a way to exist as one of the community. Which lead to his first predicament. Not only would he have to deceive the woman he refused now to think as anything more than a target, he would have to present himself as a man of the cloth, as humans called their Catholic priests.

Sabian shook his head, hoping Celestia's focus was fully on the road she navigated. He was in the most awkward of positions. This woman, designed for higher purpose, had captured something from within him he hadn't known existed. That thing, that *needing*, that overwhelming want to protect, was not his to desire nor hers to covet. It irritated his system that those feelings remained once his memory returned.

As a vessel to produce future warriors for the King of Kings, as the life-mate to a well-deserving warrior and son of a repentant angel, Celestia would be held in the highest esteem, though Sabian doubted she'd know it or care. Her destiny was the ultimate function a human could achieve in the angelic realm. She had the opportunity to serve The Master with pure intent. Sabian was trying hard to remember that, not resent losing what was never meant for him to have.

And yet he coveted her.

There was nothing he could do but proceed. And do so as quickly as possible. Once he was done with this chore, he could go back to the existence he'd always known and forget about *feelings*....

"Sabastian, we're almost to the base of the mountain. I want to go by my clinic first. I can charge my phone there while making sure I don't have any patients waiting. We can use the landline to call the church and see if they were expecting you. Although I doubt anyone has been out and about this early in the morning."

Sabian nodded. "That's fine. I have nowhere to be."

He frowned, knowing every word henceforth would be its own deception. He'd be a liar, a cheat, he'd commit fraud, and he'd kill, because he had to! Angry, but refusing to be sickened by the directive to break every law known to his kind, Sabian steeled himself to dig into the act, even to the point of mentally calling himself Sabastian over and over again. The last thing he needed to do was slip up. Until he found that as-yet-unknown woman destined for death, he knew he'd have to court the one sitting next to him while still holding *her* at a distance. As much as he wished it for Celestia, he couldn't afford to have her drop him off somewhere and put him out of her life.

"Are you hungry?"

Since they hadn't taken the time to eat, and his human stomach was grinding, it was a relief to be able to be honest about one thing. "I could eat."

She glanced over at him, making him realize his tone was too curt. Sabian looked back with what he was certain would be flirty eyes. "I'm definitely hungry."

He must have overdone it. Celestia's brows drew together, and her eyes blink rapidly.

"Me too. I'm sorry we had to leave so quickly. But we need to find out who you are, and I have a business to run."

He nodded. Even though he'd decided his plan of action, he wasn't entirely sure how to proceed. It had been easier when he'd had no memories. Then he could act normally on the attraction he felt for Celestia. Now he had to walk a fine line. He couldn't anger those watching him, and he had to find a way to make her want to be with him as much as possible while searching for the one meant to die.

"Are you okay?"

His gaze flew to hers where he again saw concern and confusion in her beautiful eyes. He was going to have to make sure to keep a mask in place at all times, otherwise his conflicting emotions were going to give him away. He grinned. "I'm great, actually. My body barely pains me, and I am in the company of a gorgeous woman. What more could a man ask for?"

Celestia's expression eased, though her lips barely lifted.

"Should you say things like that?"

Sabian pushed out a breath, not wanting it to be the focus of her attention. "I don't think I'm a priest," he confessed, feeling it necessary to get her off that track. The last thing he wanted to do was end up taking the church community on this ride of deception. He'd have to come up with another way.

Her raised brows slid back down as she turned her attention to the ribbon of road taking them around the large lake once they finally reached the valley. "But you were so sure last night."

Her features were neutral in profile, as if she were purposefully not looking at him or willing to share her thoughts. He swallowed, hating what he was doing to her, knowing what he had yet to do would hurt her even more.

He had no choice. None. Not if he wanted to continue existing. He would have to lull her into a state of acceptance of her fate, but there was no way to do that without first making her want to go with him. As he thought about it, it was clear he'd have to make her think everything he did was about wanting her for himself. Once accomplished, he'd have to hand her over to another. She would hate him for all of eternity. And it would be no more than he deserved.

His gut burned, twisted, replacing the hunger he'd felt

only moments before. Shaking off the anger building inside, he turned to look out of the window at his side. The snow-covered trees and flatter landscape was another reminder of the world from which he came. He swallowed again, this time against the knot building in his throat. He fought against the liquid flooding his eyes, and knew, in that moment, and for the first time in his existence, his heavenly home was not the only place filled with beauty. The Creator had made the earth so perfect. Though no longer what it once was, there were places, like Mystic Waters, where those who took care of the land did so with great concern and care.

"We can grab something to eat on the way to the clinic. It's a little out of the way but no problem."

Sabian turned back to find Celestia studying him. "That sounds good."

She nodded and took a turn, but he didn't pay attention to their route. He focused on the snow blanketed row of houses they passed and found himself looking at each facing window, as if he'd be able to see those inside.

It occurred to him he was already looking for the woman he was meant to kill, although there was no chance, without his angelic supremacies, he'd be able to penetrate those walls. The burdens of being human, he decided, were going to be many.

They pulled up to a large sign with food pictured on it, and Celestia asked what he wanted. It took a few moments to read all the options, before he settled on a couple of sandwiches the breakfast menu displayed. Celestia ordered, moved forward to pay for their meals, and then was handed a white paper bag. Drinks with tops and straws were next, each of which she held out to him to hold.

"We'll eat when we get to the clinic."

Sabian nodded, not responding to her clipped words. He could tell by her tone she was irritated with him or something. He didn't know what to do about that either and was afraid to say or do much until he figured out how to proceed. He knew he'd have to do something quickly, or she was likely to send him on his way.

It took only moments before she was turning into a large driveway and a Mystic Waters Veterinary Clinic sign indicated they'd reached their destination. She turned off her truck and reached for one of the two drinks he held in his hands. Sabian refused to release it.

"I want you."

Celestia's gaze flew from the drink to meet his, her filled with questions.

"You are confusing me."

Shame filled him. The new emotion was one he didn't like. "I know, and I'm sorry. I'm trying to be fair"—*liar*—"and not do anything or rush into anything you'll later regret." Liar!

Her expression transformed before his eyes to one of sweetness. "I'm sorry. I know you aren't sure of anything right now. I shouldn't place my concerns on you as well. It's just that there is something about you that calls to me."

She shook her head in sharp little bursts. "I know that makes no sense."

It did. That was the problem. Not only did he want her to want to be with him, her destiny was to be with one like him, even though she didn't know it yet. That was what she was feeling, he was certain. He could do nothing but use it to his advantage.

"It does. Something about you calls to me as well."

That her eyes now shown with relief only served to dig deeper into his soul. She was too good for the lot of them, he decided, but that wasn't his decision to make. Just move it forward. Whether the voice was his own, or the Master's order, Sabian wasn't sure, but it didn't matter. "I don't know who I am, but I do know I want to be with you, as I have never wanted another."

Truth finally.

Dirty.

Filthy.

Truth.

She leaned across the seat toward him and Sabian didn't stop her. When her lips lightly brushed his, the needs of his head and heart smacked against each other viciously, taking his breath. Her gentle smile as she moved away indicated she took that stuttering reaction as passion, when in fact it was nothing more than self-loathing. But the game had begun, and he had to win.

Or all was lost.

Chapter Ten

"Do you know yet, when you're coming home?"

Just hearing her mother's voice brought relief in so many ways—but more concerns as well. Haven's tone was solemn while Celestia shared a minimal amount of information about what had transpired over the past couple of days. Mostly her sadness radiated concern over all that was happening in Gavin's life. His wife was in the later stages of a fight with pancreatic cancer major surgery hadn't cured, and her mortal life about to end. To top it off, their son was acting out his anger in ways that had landed the child in major trouble with the law.

Celestia heard the heartbreak in her mother's voice as she admitted her mystical healing powers hadn't been able to repair the ravaged body. The spread of disease was too advanced by the time they'd known about it. And they'd arrived too late for her to have any possibility of turning the tide. Since Haven could do nothing more than ease the poor woman's pain, they'd all had to accept this was one of those times death was meant to win. But the burdens and sorrows didn't stop there.

While Haven consoled Gavin and stood vigil over his wife, the rest of the family was desperately trying to pull strings to keep the juvenile justice system from taking Gavin's child and incarcerating him for the next couple of years. It was rare her family went up against the laws of the land, but these were extenuating circumstances.

Having heard about her cousin and his problems, and everything they were all dealing with, Celestia felt ridiculous for bothering her mother at all.

She was an adult. And needed to handle this herself.

"I don't. Unless you need me right this minute, we have to stay and see all this through."

"Of course you do! I'm fine. Everything here is fine. I just wanted to let you know about the blizzard, and that the horses are fine, mostly."

"There's more. I can hear it in your voice."

Celestia debated and then smiled a little to herself. "I think my gift might be manifesting. But it's only little things, and I don't know for sure if it's really anything."

"That's wonderful! Tell me what's happening!"

Since her mother's voice now held joy, Celestia pressed forward. "I talked to Sapphire and touched her, and something happened. I don't even know how to describe it, but it was like what I was saying was truth."

"About her babies?"

Celestia's surprise lasted only a second. Of course, Haven and her sisters knew. They were The Three, and nothing got past them when they were around their children. "Well, yes. But she didn't want me to say anything."

A small chuckle came across the call. "I know. Destiny picked up on it last time they were together. Rayne asked us not to say anything either, until Sapphire is ready to let us know. So your secret is safe with me. But tell me, what did you say? And how did it make you feel?"

She hurriedly relayed the encounter, and then her sense of serenity. Now was not the time to go into more. "I'll let you get back, Mom. I know don't want to be away from Gavin and Vivian for too long. Let us know how everything is going, as you can."

"I will, baby. Tell everyone there to send good thoughts in this direction. Gavin is going to need all the support he can get."

"I will. Love you!"

"Love you, too."

The call ended and Celestia lowered the phone to her chest, only to realize how heavy her heart felt from within.

"Is everything okay?"

She glanced back to find Sabastian standing in the doorway to the examining room. "My cousin's wife is dying. She's still so young. And has a family."

His brows flicked then smoothed out. "It is the way of life."

Since his reaction wasn't the usual platitude, she frowned. "Yes. It is. But that's an unusual thing to say. And, since this means something to me, it's a little insulting."

Sabastian's lips pursed, before he shrugged, and spoke. "It simply is. I didn't mean to make it sound so callus."

Somewhat mollified, Celestia walked toward him. "I would ask if there was anyone you wanted to call, but you said you don't want to think about going to the church yet."

"No. I don't."

Celestia swallowed hard. The look in his eyes made her freeze in place. She swallowed again. "What do you want to do?"

"I want to kiss you."

It should have made her mad. Or frightened, since her body was jumping with joy on the inside. But the shaking within had nothing to do with either of those things. She should have wanted to deny him simply because he was confusing her, interested one minute, and pulling back the next, but she didn't. All other considerations aside, she wanted to kiss him too. More than anything.

She took a step toward him, studying the daring in the ocean of his eyes. Celestia felt her lips lifting, and as she took the last step right before him, she tilted her head back. "Then kiss me."

Every nerve tingled, every hair follicle raised in delight. Celestia let herself go, unleashing the restraints she'd started building at a very young age. She pushed the threats of reality from her mind and concentrated on the magical dance playing out between their lips.

He tasted so good and felt so right, where her length pressed tightly to his. His secure, almost crushing hold gave security she didn't know she so desperately needed. His ravaging mouth pulled moans of desire from lips they could not pass. And her mind swirled in ecstasy, as visions of galaxies flashed throughout her mind.

Sabastian eased the kiss but only allowed her to pull back enough that they could again drown in each other's eyes. "I can't let you go."

Her heart soared, even knowing she was walking on dangerous ground. She wouldn't think about repercussions, not now, not this minute. Celestia knew, with all she was, she was meant to be with this man. That knowledge was as assured and strong as when she'd spoken to Sapphire, giving Celestia confidence her gift was in indeed manifesting.

If Sabastian once had a higher calling, then it was his decision, not hers, if it no longer was. The split seconds pang was unwelcome and spoke of denial, but she would not allow regret move in and settle. She couldn't let it. Not when he said he couldn't let her go. It had to mean…all she felt was right.

****

Sabian pulled her to him again and held her close. He shouldn't have said the words aloud. He hadn't even meant to think them, much less say them. The Creator knew his heart, so there was nothing he could do about what he thought. What was worse than the possibility of getting stricken by The Master was seeing the hope of a *forever after* in Celestia's eyes.

He had no idea at this point if it was another form of punishment to witness the beginnings of love, firsthand, or if this was what all humans felt when they found that person some believed completed them.

He closed his eyes and just held on, knowing he had to go with the opportunity given him. Sabian squeezed her tightly and then grasped her shoulders to separate her body from his own. He needed her to want him close, and the pleasure having her there was painfully delicious, but he couldn't stop himself from still trying to push her away. "I don't even have a home, that I know of. You're taking a big risk opening your heart to me."

Her smile was gentle but assured. "Would it help you any if I said none of that matters to me, as long as your heart is free? Mine has already opened to yours, so what is done there is done. The question is, then, what will you do with it?"

Hesitation in reacting was there but resignation as well. He would have to use her budding feelings for him. "You barely know me."

"You know, as odd as it seems in such a short acquaintance, I do feel a special connection. I'm told it works that way sometimes. Some people call it love at first sight. But for me, it goes deeper than that.

"I'm not foolish. I know there are hurdles to overcome and bridges to cross: your loss of memory, possible emotional or contractual connections, and there are things on my side as well. My family is large, powerful, and very protective. My father and mother will want to know everything about you, and you having no idea who you are will make them suspicious. We'll have to simply work through these things a step at a time.

"Starting with the easiest. I still think we need to go to the church and make enquiries. If you are a priest, there has to be a record of it somewhere. I know you don't want to know. But I do."

Sabian felt his face contort. "There won't be anything to find," he stated, defiant.

Instantly sharp pain hit his chest with such blunt force, it knocked him back a step. Celestia moved to him quickly, and grasped both arms. "What's wrong? Are you okay? You're so pale! I'll call an ambulance! This is all too much after your injuries!"

"No, no, please. I'm fine."

It was difficult to get the words past lungs that seemed to have collapsed. But he didn't want to be examined by a medical team. He had no idea if anything about him still held angelic properties, and it wouldn't help his cause to find out the hard way. He pulled himself up straight, and Celestia released him. "I'm fine. I'm not sure what happened. But I'm fine. Let's make that call, and see what we can find out."

The call led to a visit to the high-ceilinged church, and the meeting with the elderly priest set in motion an enquiry Sabian knew was a waste of everyone's time. But the exercise served its purpose. It distracted Celestia from making more of his reaction to disobeying a direct order not to reveal angelic truths. Since the pain hadn't returned, Sabian figured it had been a small warning. This time.

Next time, he'd likely be struck by lightning...or worse.

With the lesson so fresh, Sabian knew he wouldn't entertain revealing himself again. Pain was one thing. No longer existing was something else. Especially, since it would make no difference in the end. If he failed in his task, another angel would come to take both the soul lost and Celestia anyway. He couldn't save either of them, only himself.

"I think I remember something."

She looked up as they were about to exit the building,

her expression guarded. "Being in the church?"

He shook his head. "No. I know I'm not a priest. And I know I'm not married or involved with anyone."

The relief in her eyes coincided with a deep breath that lifted and lowered her chest noticeably. The man in him noticed every nuance of the movement, and he allowed it to lead him into the next lie. "I'm a construction worker."

A laugh of delight fled from between her lips. "That's wonderful! What else do you remember?"

Sabian shook his head, not wanting to say too much. The more he lied, the more he'd have to remember later. "Nothing really."

"Not where you're from? Or who your family is?"

He waited only a heartbeat before answering. Of course, if he'd remembered anything, it would be those things. "I'm from Alaska. I came here looking for my family." At her raised brows, he hurried on. "My real family. I was adopted, and once my mother died, I decided to find my roots. So I came here."

Celestia nodded slowly. "That explains your presence in Mystic Waters, but why on the mountain, and why were you naked and injured?"

Sabian had forgotten that. "I don't remember that part. I'm still trying to work it all out."

"Oh, my!" the priest called, hurrying back over to them. "Before you go, I just got word this morning Alice Fairfield passed away. She lives right next to your vet clinic doesn't she, Ms. Hansen?"

Celestia gasped. "She does! That's awful!"

The priest nodded solemnly for a few seconds, but his eyes lit up as he turned them on Sabian. He leaned forward, his hands clasped together, and he grinned, as if dying to convey exciting news. Sabian took an instinctive step back, and then felt foolish. "What is it, Father?"

"My son! It must be God's will that you've found your

way here to see me today. Alice revealed to me Saturday last how she was excitedly anticipating the arrival of a young man she'd wanted to meet for years. Alice's daughter gave her newborn over to adoption twenty-six years ago. This man, Alice's long-lost grandchild, was expected a couple of days ago. But he never showed up. *You* never showed. We all figured it was because of the snow storm." He shook his head. "If only Alice could have held on just a little longer! She wanted to meet you so badly."

Celestia turned to Sabian, excitement and sorrow in her eyes. "I'm *so* sorry about your grandmother, but maybe now you can find her daughter! Your birthmother!"

Before he could deny they were the ones he'd been looking for, the priest spoke.

"I'm afraid not. Alice's daughter died in childbirth, and she wasn't able, or willing, to take on her newborn grandson. So she gave the child up."

"The father," Sabian asked, hoping against hope he knew the answer.

"Never knew who he was. The daughter never told Alice as far as I know. They barely had a relationship by the time the baby was born."

It was all too perfect. Too handy. But time held no meaning in the angelic realm, and all he was experiencing now could have been in the works for human decades. Knowing he'd have to take the opportunity as offered, Sabian adopted a disappointed pose.

"Well, I guess that's that then."

The priest shook his head. "Alice would have had a will. She spoke of it after her daughter died. Since she wasn't here to inherit the little the woman owned, she was going to leave it to the child. All you have to do is find it and claim your birthright.

"Do you still want me to make inquiries of the church about you?"

Sabian shook his head. "No. There's no point. But thank you for your time. And the information."

"Not at all. I am sorry you never got a chance to know your grandmother. She was quite a character."

****

The house was filthy, but it was his.

At least everyone insisted that to be true.

Fortunately, or unfortunately, depending on perspectives, Celestia had often checked on the elderly woman and had a spare key at her clinic, which simplified them getting in Alice's house. Now that he saw what a hoarder's residence looked and smelled like from the human perspective, he wasn't sure there was any way he could stay.

"We need to open windows."

He glanced down to find Celestia looking around; her expression of distaste and disgust matched his own.

"I guess this is why she always walked over to the clinic to get the groceries I bought her. She'd never let me deliver them to the house."

"But she gave you a key."

Celestia nodded. "She said I could only use it if I didn't hear from her for days. That if she died in there, and no one found her after too long, that the house would stink unmercifully."

They shared a look. Neither said a word.

Sabian shrugged. "I guess I'd better get those windows open."

Celestia moved forward with him.

"No, you shouldn't be in here. Give me a few days to clean it out. Then I'll invite you back over. I'd rather only one of us get rat-bitten."

She looked up at him, but hurt replaced the relief he expected to see.

"You don't want my help?"

He smiled, wishing he could say yes. But he wasn't going to subject her to his punishment. At least not yet. "I don't want you to have to deal with this. You have a business to run. But I wouldn't mind taking meals with you—elsewhere, while I'm working this out."

Now he saw the relief in her smile.

"Absolutely. I'm moving into the clinic, which basically means I'm moving the rest of my clothes from my house to the apartment above the clinic. I'll have breakfast ready first thing in the morning, if you want to come over early. I don't open the doors until nine, unless there's an emergency. And I haven't gotten any calls about appointments for today yet, either. This snow has everyone staying home, if they can. Not everyone knows the clinic is back open. It was closed after the last vet retired a few months ago."

Her quick words had Sabian wondering if she was anxious to get away from the disaster piled around them, and him as well, now that she could. At the same time, it was clear she wanted to see him as soon as possible, and though it was wrong, he knew he'd be counting the hours as well. There was nothing about any of this that made any sense at all.

She shouldn't want to be with him and he couldn't want to be with her.

Obviously, he was losing the human mind he'd been handed.

Sabian was sure this was *another* in the long line of punishments he was to endure before this journey to redemption ended.

"So," she continued, "if you want, I can still help. I'll just have to find a hazardous materials suit first! You'll need one and cleaning supplies too. Until you can get your feet under you, the meals are on me. Let's leave this for now, and get something to eat, and go shopping. This place has bleach and trash bags written all over it. Once we start carrying things out, we can fill my truck, and take everything to the dump."

She said the last with a laugh, and the part of him that wanted her close for himself wanted to accept her offer. But he knew he had to deny that part. As much as he could. As for the rest, he was at her mercy. With nothing but human abilities, he was stuck.

"Let's play it by ear. For now, before I touch anything in here, let's get that food and the cleaning supplies, but I want to keep track of everything you spend. Once I'm in a position to repay you, I will."

Celestia flapped a hand at him. "It isn't an issue."

"It is to me."

She grinned. "I like a man with pride."

Though his face responded in kind, he cringed inwardly. He wasn't a man. Not really. And his words, though he'd meant them as they left his lips, were hollow. Once it was all done, he wouldn't be looking for a job to repay her, he'd be taking away the life she had. It was a bitch that a human conscience came with the human body and mind.

Chapter Eleven

Celestia sat across from Sabastian and chewed slowly. There was such peace in finding someone to share a meal with, to have easy conversation with, to desire. He was so beautifully made. Masculine with hard angles and large tightly sculptured muscles that moved and flexed when he was in motion, without him even being aware. His curiosity at the things he touched, whether his bear-handled fork when he lifted it or the restaurant's mountain-country designs and furnishings, gave her a settled feeling that had been lacking in her life so far.

Soft Irish flutes played from the speakers quietly, not overpowering conversation, but enhancing the atmosphere, making the rough-and-tumble décor dreamier than it should have. Or maybe it was because she was falling in love.

Of course, that was frightening. Terrifying really. Not because she feared taking him from a higher purpose, now, but because he really was available for her to pursue. It was a little embarrassing to realize. She's always hoped for the one meant to be hers. She'd fantasized about what it would be like to be able to claim him. To be able to touch and taste him at will. But now the moment was upon her, not all her nervous energy was from desire.

She was scared.

Afraid to commit herself to a life with someone else in it. She'd always been free to pursue her own dreams and desires. To take on another's would change everything. And, knowing she had to be honest, she wanted him to desire her back of his own will. Not because he was destined to be hers, but because he really wanted to love her.

There were so many things she didn't understand about the claiming the women of her family experienced. All she knew was it was there, within them, and once it happened, the man they chose would belong to them until one or the other died.

For millennia, the Cavanaugh women in her line had found their one, only to lose them shortly after. Her mother and aunts had broken that love curse before Celestia's birth, and now the pairings were lasting lifetimes. But was it fair to the men they chose? Had they really had any choice in the matter? Would Sabastian, if she said those simple words?

I claim you.

She wouldn't do it. Not until he wanted her for a lifetime first. She wanted to give him freedom of choice, knowing, if he didn't choose her, she would be forever alone.

Because there was only one.

"You're very quiet."

Celestia realized she was staring straight at Sabastian but not seeing anything, until he spoke. A shaggy breath escaped, and she smiled. "I'm thinking about us." She looked at him, now delving into his eyes. "About if there is going to be an us."

His hesitation in responding deflated everything within her, until he seemed to shake something off, and smiled so brightly, she couldn't help but hope.

"There is an us. And there always will be. I plan to be on your mind for the rest of your life."

Celestia laughed, she couldn't help it. "That's such a relief. I know you are attracted to me, but for me, it goes so much deeper."

The light in his eyes flatlined. "I am more than

attracted to you, too. I want you for all eternity. But there are things…."

He said the words with such sad sincerity that tears flooded her eyes. "You make that sound like a bad thing, but I understand your hesitancy. We have time to get to know each other now, and just knowing how you feel makes time easy to give. I know you're worried about starting over a new life and not being able to handle everything on your own yet, but those things are just things, and they'll take care of themselves."

She said no more as he nodded slowly. She wouldn't mention she was in a position to take care of them both financially while he got his life together. He was too much of a man to allow that to pass without denting him. So she changed the subject. "Let's get out of here and get to the store. I've made a mental list of everything you'll need to start decontaminating that house. Once we get all that, go with me to my house to get the clothes I need to take as well. We'll set up my apartment this evening, if you don't mind, and you can hit your house first thing in the morning. There's no way you can sleep there tonight."

Sabastian nodded and began to rise. "Can you give me a minute?"

She smiled up at him, glad he needed a reason to escape. As he headed to the sign reading Restrooms, she waved to the waitress and quickly paid the bill. At least this one time he would be spared the embarrassment she knew his lack of resources caused him.

Nearly an hour later she had no choice but to pay for the cart full of things they'd picked up in his presence. She hated that he wouldn't look at her or the woman who relayed the total. She hadn't meant to make it uncomfortable for him, but he'd needed clothing of his own, and she'd practically forced him to try on several pairs of jeans and shirts against his will. She'd judged what size boxers he'd need by his jeans size, and packages of socks by the shoes she'd insisted on as well. Celestia hadn't given him a choice in shampoo or bath soaps, not because she cared what he used, but simply to keep it from making him even more uncomfortable. She had ample supplies of those her uncle Tom's family produced at her home. She would take the lot to the clinic for herself and share with him. The cleaning supplies, the boxes of garbage bags, and the implements to hold or use with each had added to the pile of purchases.

As they pushed the cart out of the store, he finally turned to her. "This is all too much to ask of you."

Celestia stopped cold, and he did as well. "One, no it isn't. Two, you need this, and I am thankful to be able to help. Three, I know you would do the same for me if our positions were reversed. Please don't make this anything more than it is."

Heat filled her face and her chest hurt. Celestia never confronted people. It wasn't something she was comfortable doing, but she couldn't let this be something that hurt their building relationship.

Sabastian moved to her side and slid his arm around her shoulders to pull her against him. The warmth of his embrace eased her, as did his words.

"All I meant is that you are too generous. I appreciate your help and your kindness. And I'll try not to look as pitifully inadequate as I feel right now."

She looked up, knowing they were standing in the middle of a parking lot and not caring. "These circumstances don't define you. I know in my heart you are a good man, not one who would use another for his own benefit."

Though she was sure he'd been about to lean down and kiss her, he simply nodded, and took the cart to move toward the truck. She followed silently, knowing there were lots more hurdles to jump before she could claim her man.

"Celestia!"

She turned back and couldn't help but smile. Amen-ra, her cousin Jewell's husband, was jogging toward her from three aisles over. He met her at the bed of the truck, and threw a quick glance in Sabastian's direction. With a quick nod, he turned back to her.

"I'm glad to see you're safe. Dia texted Jewell last night and they were at it for hours. Talking about Ryan and Dia and the baby and your parents' trip, and who knows what else. But no one could get you, and we were all worried."

"I'm fine. I was at Mom and Dad's."

"I know. That's where Dia said she left you. Why haven't you contacted anyone?"

She hugged her cousin-in-law and stepped back. "I'm sorry. So much has gone on in the last couple of days, mostly this weather and a dead phone battery. I did talk to Sapphire briefly, though, and she knew I was okay."

Amen-ra frowned. "No one has heard from her either. But she's probably been working. I think she's gone back to the night shift. Something strange is going on around the mountain, and they asked her to." He slid an uneasy glance at Sabastian and then sent her a pointed look.

Since it was obvious he couldn't talk in from of Sabastian, it had to have something to do with magic. She nodded. "I'll call the family as soon as I can. Right now I need to get these things home, and settled." She turned to Sabastian and held out her hand, when he moved forward and took it she turned back to Amen-ra. "This is Sabastian Envoy. He's new to Mystic Waters."

Amen-ra held out his hand and they shook. "Nice to meet you. I'm Amen-ra. A cousin by marriage."

"You as well."

An awkward moment passed, and Celestia knew each man was sizing up the other. She cleared her throat. "Well, it is cold, and we need to get going. Would you tell Jewell I'm fine and I'll be in touch? We have a lot to do this afternoon, so it may be later today or tomorrow."

"Will do. You be careful."

The subtle warning was as much for Sabastian as for herself, Celestia was sure. She simply smiled, thinking it fun to be the center of two very large men's attention and concern. "I will, you too. This snowstorm has made conditions dangerous to travel in. Give Jewell my love— and the babies too."

Amen-ra raised a brow at her diversion tactics as his lips split into a miniscule smile. "I will."

He headed toward the store, and Celestia figured the ancient Egyptian had been completely domesticated by her cousin at this point. He now drove, shopped, and there was no doubt, adored not only her cousin, but all the little babies they'd produced together as well, since his move to the here and now.

She glanced at Sabastian, to find him following Amen-ra's progress. When he looked back at her, he shrugged. "Big guy."

Celestia nodded, not about to inform him Amen-ra had once been a minor Egyptian prince and palace guard, thousands of years before. Though his features still held nobility of heritage, his modern haircut, style of dress and overall easy manner, most of the time, was a far cry from the man the family first met. His original bossy-brute attitude was now replaced with a kind gentleness of spirit that made her cousin one very happy woman.

And that's all she wanted, too, Celestia admitted to herself. Someone who made her life as complete as Amen-ra was making Jewell's, Nicolae was making Sapphire's, and Zeb was making Luna's. Before too long, Dia and Ryan would live in their own perfect union, too. As did their respective parents.

"Celestia? The truck is loaded, and the cart put away. Are you ready to go?"

Feeling ridiculous for having spent time wishing on stars rather than being helpful, she nodded and rounded the truck. Sabastian beat her to the door, opened it and waited until she was inside. She looked at him, and he her, until they both smiled. His expression changed, and he moved forward. Before giving herself a chance to think, she grasped his collar and pulled him to her. Their lips met, lingered, and mingled with a slowness that only made her want more. He pulled back slowly, hesitantly, as if waiting for something to happen. With a loud breath, he stood up straight and then backed away to close the door. She had no idea why she felt he'd been waiting for something... And the only thing she could think of was lightning to strike.

But not in a good way.

****

Between the acquiring and transporting and the rearranging and sorting of supplies and possessions, Sabian was relieved they were too busy to talk about anything personal. He'd needed the time to think about what hadn't happened when he'd kissed her. Had the Creator decided to give him free rein to accomplish his goals, as long as he didn't reveal who he actually was, or his purpose for being there? Or was it just wishful thinking that he could kiss and touch Celestia as he so desired, as long as he never stepped over the bounds of actually mating with her?

From what little he believed he knew of those women destined for the Brotherhood of the Repentant, Sabian was pretty sure they could only be taken and used if pure of spirit and untouched in the ways of procreation. He had no idea how much life experience each could experience prior to that union, or why it now seemed the women with the silver blood were getting so hard to find. Those issues were never his to know as a Reaper, and what little he'd learned since falling from grace was barely enough to give him confidence to move in any direction. *But...*if he was given this small gift, this opportunity to steal moments of what he was afraid had already turned into love on his part, did he dare? Was it fair?

Nothing about what was coming Celestia's way was fair.

She would be little more than a slave to the chosen angelic warrior she'd been designed for, thousands of years before her own birth. She would have no freedom of choice. No say in her own life or that of the children she'd bear. Her sole purpose would be to serve and thus save whichever of the Brotherhood was blessed enough to warrant her as his mate. She would increase his power, provide The Master with future angelic warriors and, as a result, help to stay the darkness now threatening to overtake the children of the original repentant angels.

It mattered not that the cause was just.

He couldn't stand the thought of another touching Celestia. But worse, he hated that she would lose everything that mattered to her.

If the only happiness he could give her was memories of truly being loved, for this brief time, then he would. And he would do the same for himself. If this was all the love either of them would ever know, for eternity, then he couldn't pass up the opportunity to build memories.

Sabastian left her to finish making her newly placed bed and went downstairs to the clinic. He knew he was walking a thin line, no matter what he did or didn't allow to happen between them. He listened as he closed the door to the stairs behind him and then looked upward. "I am falling in love with her. Or I have already fallen. And I am certain she is as well. I know I have no right to ask, but I am, please, just give us time. Give me time. To give her happiness. To give her something to hold onto when her life is taken into your service.

"I don't ask this for myself. I know I will live an eternity with loss. But I will once again be upon my path. Hers will be forever changed."

There was no answer, not that he'd expected one. But there wasn't a sudden storm raging outside either, so that was something. Sabian licked his dry lips and then lowered his head to look around the sterling clean room she used to end the suffering of animals.

He thought it ironic, sad even, such a big-hearted woman would chose a career that eventually ended in souls leaving a body, when his entire existence was about the same thing. But their somewhat-parallel worlds would end soon. If he pleased The Creator, he would go back to transporting souls from the planet, and she would be bringing them into it.

The sound of her footsteps coming down the stairs propelled Sabian into motion. He was going to test the waters, going to give in and do what he desired above all else, and see if his theory was right. He swung the door open and grasped her before her foot hit the third step, to pull her into his arms. Celestia gasped as she reached out to anchor herself, but she need not have bothered. He held her against him, her feet dangling, as he ravaged the soft mouth.

She didn't fight him. Instead, she held him tighter, as her tongue wrestled with his. He slid one hand lower, then the other, clasping butt cheeks as her legs lifted and wrapped around his hips. He knew she could feel the swell of his manhood, knew too it was going to kill him to never put it to use.

She lifted one hand to slide her fingers into his hair, hard against his scalp. The other was still locked around his shoulder, until he lifted her higher, and she secured that arm around his neck.

Celestia tore her mouth from his, her harsh breaths blowing his face. The hunger in her eyes was nearly his undoing, but the sensations when she spoke nearly took him to his knees.

"I claim you!"

Thunder cracked and the room darkened, the floor beneath his feet shifted, popping shiny porcelain tiles from their spot, and he had to hold her tighter as he spread his legs to keep from falling. He shifted her so he was grasping her hips, allowing her feet to hit the floor, afraid he'd feel the deathblow at any moment. If he was to be taken out because of his blunder, he didn't want her to get hurt as well.

But the house settled, the room lightened, and he looked down to see her gazing up with fear. She shook her head, and took a step back. "I can explain that."

Sabian frowned, not knowing what to say to the desperation in her voice. He'd been ready to make all kinds of crazy cracks about sudden snowstorms and destructive earthquakes in the area, but now he was too curious to utter a word.

She grinned, sheepishly. "We have crazy storms and earthquakes here. They strike at the oddest times."

****

Celestia hoped her sudden inspiration camouflaged the fact her claiming had resulted in such a wild reaction. In a way it made her want to jump with joy, since it was yet again another indication she was coming into her mystical being. On the other hand, she was going to have to be very careful. If strange things started happening because of her changing, then he might start asking questions. None of which she could answer yet.

At least, not until her mother could advise her.

If it were only herself, it would be a simple matter. She'd take the chance he'd have trouble accepting her mystical side. But it wasn't. She had to take into consideration how revealing herself would affect the rest of the family. Which left nothing to do but keep on pretending what had just happened wasn't because of her.

"Are you okay?"

Sabastian nodded. "I'm fine. You?"

She nodded as well, now not sure how to proceed. Their moment of intense passion was over, and reigniting it seemed silly, given the mess at their feet. "I guess I need to clean this up. And I'll have to get someone to replace the tiles. I can't have anyone tripping on them."

Sabastian immediately dropped to his haunches and began picking up the sharp pieces. She did the same, feeling lost, until they reach for the same shard, and their hands touched. He looked up as she did, and their eyes met. His smile bloomed first, and there was no way she could stop hers following. He placed his fingers over her knuckles. "Let me get this. Can you get something to put them in?"

Celestia's breath rattled in her chest. Just the touch of his hand did that. She wanted to tell him to forget it and take her into his arms again, but he was already busily piling up the bits and pieces that once was her floor. She rose and rounded the table she'd put the little Chihuahua to sleep on, to grasp the small trashcan she used for non-biohazard waste. That only forty-eight hours had passed since Chili Pepper was in the room, taking her last breath, seemed surreal. It felt like a lifetime had passed.

Celestia carried the can and sat it down next to the piled tiles. "I'll get the vacuum for the dust and tiny pieces."

Sabastian nodded without looking up. She turned away and headed to what she'd deemed the janitor's closet.

They worked in silence until the floor, if not intact, was at least clean. As the last of the supplies were put away, and the garbage set at the side door for disposal in the morning, Celestia's nerves increased.

They hadn't spoken of the kiss, the earthquake or her declaration, but now that there was nothing left to distract, she didn't know how to proceed. When Sabastian seemed at a loss as well, she moved forward and placed her hands on his biceps. "Stay with me tonight? In my bed?"

His expression wasn't one she expected, and her nerve dissolved.

"Please don't do that."

She searched his eyes. "Do what?"

"Look like I've disappointed you. I want to say yes."

"Then say yes."

His smile was gentle and somewhat sad.

"I don't think it's a good idea. I don't want to rush this."

Ah... "I don't feel rushed."

Sabastian's chuckle was filled with self-derision.

"I need to go slower. There are things I need to know...about myself."

He looked away, and she felt bad about putting him on the spot. He'd only just found his family, only to find them gone from his life for good. "I'm sorry about your grandmother. And you're right. You need some time to get this all straight in your mind. But I want you to know something. I'm here. And I'm not going anywhere."

Chapter Twelve

It was a relief to have Sabastian next door busily beginning the process of cleaning out his house. The night turned awkward after their chat about being a couple, and he'd slept on the couch rather than in her bed. Then he'd been in such a hurry to get started this morning he'd barely said two words to her before hitting the door.

It was just as well. They both had things to do, and he needed space. Celestia blew out a breath, determined not to let it bother her… *much*.

An Irish tune, indicating her next youngest sister was calling, sounded. Celestia snatched the phone up, relieved something other than Sabastian would occupy her mind, if only briefly.

"Mom and Dad are heading home day after tomorrow," Soleli stated, without preamble.

Celestia couldn't help but smile. Her sister never wasted time on frivolous talk. "And good morning to you too."

There was slight pause, and then Soleli chuckled. "Yeah, sorry. Good morning. I just got a call from Mom. The news is bad. Vivian passed away last night."

Deciding the niceties had ended, she clutched the phone harder. "I'm so sorry to hear that."

It was sadder still she felt nothing more than a distant sorrow for the woman her cousin married. The truth was, she barely knew her or their son for that matter. Other than a few brief family trips to California when she was younger, there hadn't been a chance to get to know any of them better. Even her cousin Gavin was more a theoretical family connection, than a real one. They were all so close, forever in each other's presence and business, but he'd avoided Mystic Waters since leaving nearly a quarter of a century before.

"Aren't they staying for the funeral?"

"There isn't going to be one. Gavin is having her cremated, and as soon as he can clear up some legalities, he's going to pack up and head back to Mystic Waters with his son.

"Mom said he'll have a memorial service here once they move in and are settled, but for now, he has to focus on his loss and his son's. It's all so terribly sad."

Celestia listened as Soleli detailed the legal problems Gavin's son, Jason, had ahead of him, even with everyone doing all they could to smooth the way. Apparently, the reality of his mother's impending death set in motion a rage the fifteen-year-old could neither handle nor contain. He'd taken a baseball bat to several very expensive cars in his high school parking lot. Jason had not only been kicked out of school, he was arrested and detained in a juvenile facility as well.

"Since Gavin and Uncle Garrison have compensated the kids' parents financially, they're dropping charges, but he still has to deal with social services. Given the circumstances, and Aunt Destiny's ability to alter feelings, it looks like they're going to let Jason move, under Gavin's supervision. But even if they do, it could take months before the Department of Children's Services releases him completely. Mom said he might have to deal with them once he gets here too."

"Poor Gavin. He must be beside himself."

"Yeah," Soleli added. "Mom says he's a complete mess."

They talked some more, about the melting snow, about the plans that were put off to celebrate Celestia's end of a very long education, and now the new job, and, finally, Soleli mentioned the one thing Celestia had hoped to avoid for a while.

"Jewell said Amen-ra saw you with a man."

Knowing she was letting silence linger too long, Celestia sighed. "Yes. He's new in town."

Again, silence.

"And?"

"And there's too much to go into and too much going on. I'd rather postpone this until I have more to say."

"So he's important?"

Her sister's perception wasn't unexpected. "He is."

"Ah...."

Celestia smiled to herself. "Yeah, ah...."

"Okay, keep your secrets. But as soon as Mom and Dad and the aunts and uncles are back, that celebration is a given. By then, you'd better have details to share."

Before Celestia could respond, Soleli continued, "Anyway, I have to go. I'm heading to the mountain to check out a cave that's supposed to have crystals Aunt Rayne wants for some spell. Mom asked if I could get them as quickly as possible, so my day off will be filled with hiking and gathering. Not that I mind. I rarely get outdoors anymore. You want to go with me?"

Celestia hesitated, tempted to leave her own problems behind. She bit her bottom lip then shook her head, even though Soleli couldn't see her. "I guess I should stay here and be available should anyone need a vet. But thanks for asking."

"Okay. I could have used the company, but I know you're trying to get the business going. It takes people time to adjust to a new doctor, whether for themselves or their pets. I'm heading out then. Talk soon."

"Okay, bye, then."

Celestia leaned back against the examining table,

hoping euthanizing the Chihuahua wasn't the first and last bit of business she would do now she was truly on her own. Assisting for the vet all those years, every chance she could, gave her insight into the level of patients she might expect, but people had found someone else in the interim apparently, so she was going to have to find a way to advertise being open for business.

The bell on the front door sent her heart racing and propelled her feet into motion. She hurried to the patient reception room, only to stop short. A very large man with curly blond hair stared back at her, with nary a pet at his side. But the most arresting thing about his astounding looks was the one-shouldered white dress he wore... Which barely passed his thick muscular thighs.

****

Sabian carried fifteen bags filled with garbage outside, deciding he'd make a pile in the back corner of the yard before having Celestia bring her truck closer. Since he had no personal attachment to any of Alice's things, cleaning out the house was going fairly quickly, though he'd barely put a dent in the first room, much less the overall job.

Since his hands were sweating from within rubber gloves he'd insisted he didn't need at the store the day before—but found he wouldn't touch a thing without today—he pulled them off and rolled them inside-out. He'd put new ones on before continuing, but he needed to spend a few minutes in the fresh morning air.

With long strides, he rounded the house, noting how much work would be required to make the yard presentable as well. At least it wouldn't stink him out as the house was doing. Even with every window open and one of Celestia's vet masks covering his mouth and nose, the smells were overwhelming. He glanced over to the building where she was setting up house and shop, wishing he could go over and try to make amends. He knew her feelings were hurt and confused, but he had no idea what to do about it.

The flash of light at her front door startled him, and then he stiffened in disbelief as the light turned into the form of a man.

Sabian took off at a run as the angel entered the front door. He wasn't supposed to be here! He wasn't supposed to take Celestia before Sabian accomplished his goals!

He made it to the door and kicked it open, only to see Celestia's stricken, frozen, terrified face. He looked around quickly, but there was no one else there.

She collapsed seconds before he could get to her. He scooped her against him and held her tightly in his arms. "What happened?"

Celestia looked up into his eyes, her own looking lost. "I don't know. There was a man. Or I thought there was. He spoke to me. Like he was angry. Then you busted the door open and he was gone."

She frowned, and shook her head. "Why did you do that? Did you know him? Did you even see him?"

Sabian didn't know how to respond. He didn't want her to think herself crazy, nor him. "What did he say?"

She shuddered so hard his fear escalated by bounds. "Tell me, Celestia!"

"He said *I was his.*"

Sabian held her tighter, his anger growing with each breath. He kissed the top of her head, and helped her to stand. Not yet! Not damned yet!

"Come with me." He half supported, half dragged her to the office chair at the reception desk and sat her down. "You stay put. I'm going to take a look around the clinic. If he's still here…" What? What could he do? He had no power against an angel who still held his angelic supremacies and no right to deny him if he'd come to collect his destined mate.

Forcing himself to cool down, Sabian stepped out of

the room and searched the others, but there was no sign of the angel. If he was still around, he wasn't making his presence known. Which, hopefully, meant the Brother had been the one to break rules this time. Since Sabian knew firsthand how badly that could turn out for the offender, he checked back in on Celestia. She seemed to have gathered herself some. "No sign of anyone."

She crossed to him. "He was real. Right?"

Sabian nodded slowly. "I saw him outside."

"But how did he get away? He was literally here one moment and gone the next."

"I can't say. But it looks like he's gone."

"Should we call the police? My cousin Sapphire is on the force. She will have everyone out searching for him. He must be crazy. Did you see his dress?"

That the angel was wearing the clothing of his heavenly rank indicated he didn't spend much time on the earth in human form. Since he couldn't explain such to Celestia, he merely smiled. "Maybe he's a cross-dresser."

She didn't catch his humor or chose to ignore it. "It was more like a costume. I think he could be dangerous, Sabastian. Really."

He nodded. "I'm going to check around outside. But keep the door open and stay where I can hear you if you yell. Do you have any patients scheduled for today?"

"Not yet. No."

"Good. Put on some old clothes and shoes you don't mind ruining. You may not want to keep anything you wear over there once this is done. I didn't want you to have to deal with it, but I need to get back to cleaning out that mess, and I'm not leaving you here alone. At least not until we know it's safe."

Celestia threw her arms around his neck and pulled him close. She placed her head on his chest. "Thank you. I didn't want to be left alone."

Sabian held her, wishing he could enjoy the feeling of her high breasts against him.

****

They cleaned for the entire day, until night fell. Amazingly, the temperatures rose drastically, which made the smell of the house worse, but it also caused the snow to melt at a rapid rate. Now that it was again cool, wearily they crossed the yard, over the small, still icy parking lot, and into the clinic. Were she not so filthy, Celestia knew she'd crawl up the stairs and fall into bed, but she felt rancid and knew Sabastian must as well.

"We should strip here, and let me throw our clothes into the clinic's washer."

Sabastian nodded. "Do you want me to give you privacy?"

She studied his tense features. "I've seen you naked."

His features eased into a grin. "That's true."

"And I'm comfortable with my body."

He looked her up and down. "I can see why."

She laughed at that, and began unbuttoning her shirt. "So why are you still just standing there?"

Sabastian hesitated and then shook his head. "Are you trying to seduce me?"

Celestia shrugged. "I'm not opposed to you doing so. But for now, I just want to get clean."

He nodded sharply, ignoring her words. "You go ahead and strip and get your shower. I'm going for a walk and will add my clothes to the washer when I get back."

Sabastian turned and left without another word. She removed her clothes, uncertain how to proceed next. She'd staked her claim. She'd declared her intentions. She'd even offered to get naked with him....

But she wasn't going to push. Though they'd done nothing more than share glances throughout the day while working, she'd gotten the impression each of his meant something. There was longing in his eyes, she was sure of it.

Or was it this longing in her heart?

Maybe she was seeing something that wasn't there. Or maybe his grief was too heavy to overcome so soon. But no matter what, she'd bound herself to him. The question was, had she made a terrible mistake?

No, she couldn't have. Surely, she wouldn't feel so strongly about him if it were a mistake. But what did she know? She'd never felt this way about anyone before. She'd witnessed blooming love, but seeing or hearing about what her cousins and sister experienced in their partnerings and living it were two completely different things.

Mom! I need you!

The sound of Soleli's cell-tune broke the silence, making Celestia jump before she quickly bent to dig the phone from the pocket of her jeans. Fleetingly she thought about being thankful for the call, since otherwise she might have thrown the phone in the washer accidentally. She punched the screen before putting it to her ear. "Hi!"

"Hi. You sound breathless. You're not in the middle of anything important, are you?"

Celestia grimaced. If only. "No, nothing going on here. Just getting ready to shower. What's up?"

"Mom called. Said she couldn't get through to you, and Aunt Destiny told her she felt you needed your mom."

Sighing with a smile, Celestia reached for the remaining clothes to carry them to the laundry. "You gotta love this family. I was just wishing Mom was here."

"Yeah, me too. I know we're grown women, but it feels strange having them so far away."

It was a relief Soleli didn't want to explore why she needed their mom. "Yes. It does."

"Well, while I was talking to her, she said we're all getting together for a cookout immediately after they get back. She said, after seeing Gavin lose his wife and, he fears, his son as well, she and the aunts want to see all their children, and she wants to go on and have that celebration for you."

"It isn't a big deal. I wish they wouldn't make one of it. And do they know about the snow?"

"It is so a big deal! You got your degree two years ahead of schedule! You've opened up your own business! I'm still struggling to get through med school. And yes to the snow. Mom's been busy from across the country. Have you seen how much has already thawed today? That wasn't without a little help from her."

Celestia frowned. She'd never heard this sudden despair in her sister's voice, nor had Soleli ever said anything negative about the career she'd wanted since they were children. "You're struggling?"

There was a moment's pause. "Yes. I haven't said anything, because I don't want to disappoint everyone. Especially Dad."

Compassion made her want to pull her sister close, but all she could do now was drop her clothes into the washer and move to the stairs. "I'm sorry you would even think such a thing. No one will be disappointed in you! We all struggle with something."

"It isn't my grades… Well, it wasn't until recently. I just feel dissatisfied with everything right now, including school. I don't know if this is what I am really supposed to be doing. But I've invested all these years, and the family has expectations. I have… *had* expectations."

The sadness in her sister's voice carried Celestia up the stairs. She wedged into the tight little bathroom, deciding immediately the design and construction members of the family were going to do a major upgrade. She was too spoiled, no doubt, to be able to accept the bathroom the way it was now. Besides, the men loved remodeling and would be happy to take care of it for her.

If only she knew the words to say to give Soleli comfort. All she came up with was, "Give yourself time to think about all of it. If you do decide it isn't what you want, then give yourself however long it takes to figure out what you do. No one will think badly of you. We all just want each other to be happy."

"I know. But I've told everyone since I was little I just wanted to be a heart surgeon like our father. And until lately, I believed it. But now, I'm not so sure."

"Has anything happened?"

The connection was silent for several seconds. When Soleli spoke, there were tears in her voice, "I'm lonely. I'm so tired of being lonely. With a family the size of ours, and everyone always around, I shouldn't feel this way! I should be thanking my lucky stars instead of pining for something I can't even grasp."

Since she understood perfectly where Soleli was coming from, she nodded. "I get it. I really do. I've been lonely, too. And I don't want to be anymore either."

"And we never got our gifts! Everyone else did but not us! What is that!" Soleli added, anger rising with each word.

Celestia couldn't say anything to that. To admit she believed hers was coming in would only hurt Soleli more at the moment, as would mentioning she'd claimed a man for her own. It just wasn't the right time to share the tentative joys trying to fill her. Nor the fears she might be wrong.

Neither spoke. Celestia could only surmise Soleli was as lost in her own confused thoughts as she was.

"Well, I'll let you go. Just be prepared to be celebrated in Cavanaugh style, day after tomorrow. The moms won't have it any other way." Soleli said, before they bid each other farewell.

There was really nothing more to say anyway. She was going to be celebrated, as her sister said, and there was nothing she could do but prepare for it. Which meant she had to find a way to explain Sabastian's sudden appearance, her falling for him, and her claiming him with no regard for the consequences should it be a mistake....

"I'm back. Are you done in there?"

Hearing Sabastian's voice set her in motion. She placed the phone on the sink's vanity and hurriedly stepped into the tub that would soon be replaced with a walk-in shower. "No! Sorry. I was on the phone with my sisters. I'll be quick!"

Chapter Thirteen

Sabian heard the water turn on and spun around quickly to flee back down the stairs and out the side door of the clinic. The part of him that instantly pictured Celestia in there, naked, rubbing soapy suds over her long form, was a side he needed to suppress instantly. The benefits of the walk he'd taken only moments before, to lecture himself about what he couldn't have and should and shouldn't do, went right out the window the minute he head her voice and visualized water running over her breasts and down her body.

Reiterating it all would be a waste of time, so he didn't bother. Begging for a different outcome than the one set in place was useless as well. He had no choice but to handle her in a way that made her want to be with him, that would make her fall so deeply in love with him she'd be willing to do anything for him. Even if it meant freely giving herself over to another and giving up all she knew. In the meantime, he desperately wanted to fulfill as many of her desires as he could for as long as they had, but he couldn't cross over that diamond hard line.

There was the matter of the other, as well. Even still given the opportunity to transport Celestia to her fated destination, it had to be after he found the woman whose soul he'd lost, and he had to make sure that one died this time. By his hands… The trouble was he had no idea where to start looking or a means to get away alone to find her. And he wasn't entirely sure he could go through with it. Of all the souls he'd transported since the beginning of mankind, he'd never been strapped with the care or concern for the deceased nor those they left behind.

Being with Celestia had changed all that. Now he had to worry over hurting her feelings, knowing she would eventually feel betrayed. He had to make her understand he had no choice, but the truth was he did. He could opt out, be no more, and none but The Creator would know he'd ever existed.

Sabian chewed at his bottom lip, and despite his inner turmoil, he focused on enjoying that no matter how small an action he performed with his human body, there was a reactive feeling. Willing to have his thoughts diverted, he focused on the touch of his hard teeth against the flesh of his lips. The sensation was an interesting one. Not as pleasant as kissing Celestia, for sure, but interesting all the same.

Although he awoke in the forest and found his first experience with physical awareness unpleasant, accepting that some type of stimulation was better than none was a no-brainer. There was such pleasure in touching, *being* touched, especially by Celestia—but pain as well. He could never relieve those pressures her touch invoked, though it was on his mind all the time… *all the time.*

There were other sensations he enjoyed that had less of an emotional impact, as when relieving his bladder or feeling the accelerated beats of his heart when he was involved in some type of physical activity. He loved the sensation of air against his skin and the refreshment of cool water sliding down his throat.

He'd miss having nerve endings once he was again nothing more than a flash of light, capable of pulling souls to their final destination. Sure, he still missed the ability to be anywhere, at any time, using nothing more than thought, as well as being free to find and deal with those things he must. Being landlocked, and body-trapped, was a handicap in so many ways. Still, if he could just have Celestia for himself, he knew he'd give up all else and turn into whatever type of man she needed.

"Sabastian? What are you doing out here?"

He turned, finding that her towel wrapped hair and housecoat-covered body did nothing to ease the desire that now seemed to have taken him completely over. He moved toward her slowly, knowing the only thing keeping him from taking her into his arms was he still smelled like a dumpster. Which was how he'd make sure he stayed. At this point, he feared it was the only way he'd get through this mess.

"I just got a call from my sister. We're going to a cookout with all my family day after tomorrow. If you want to go. You don't have to go with me if you don't want to, but I'd like for you to, if you do."

He didn't, but he would.

Meeting her family would only make it harder to take her away when the time came. But it was his first opportunity to start getting a look around Mystic Waters. If they drove through downtown, he'd scour the streets looking for the woman he'd lost. The chances of it being so easy were slim, he knew, but he had to start somewhere.

"That would be great." He smiled at her and knew himself for a gigantic fraud. "I need to hit the shower and then your couch. I want to get an early start tomorrow and get as much done as I can since we'll be busy the day after."

Celestia tried to hide it, but he could see the disappointment on her face. "Do you want me to help again? And don't you want something to eat?

Sabian nodded. Having her close again all day would be torture in many ways, but he didn't want to take a chance the angel might appear and he'd not be close enough to intervene, if that were even possible. "If you don't have anything to do here. I could use the help."

"I still don't have any appointments. I can leave a note

on the door saying I'm right next door if anyone shows up." Her face contorted. "And if that man comes back… We got so busy earlier, I forgot to call Sapphire."

Not wanting her to think about that, he stepped closer, and although he hadn't meant his scent being the thing that distracted her, her wrinkled nose and indrawn brows gave him something to work with. "I'll get cleaned up, and I could use a little something to eat."

She smiled. "I have stuff to make sandwiches and a salad in the refrigerator. It isn't much."

"Anything is fine. Just let me get this stink off me first."

He climbed in the shower, relived to see she'd already laid everything out for him. The new clothes Celestia helped him pick out during the rather interesting shopping trip were lying neatly on her bed. Unlike the coveralls he'd spent the day in, the jeans and button-down shirt looked comfortable, and it would be nice to wear something that actually fit. He'd stripped quickly downstairs and left the boots they'd purchased there as well. It was a good thing. He'd hated to have whatever germs attached to them jumping off to live in the plush carpeting of her apartment.

It was something, what these humans did to assure their comfort and entertainment. She hadn't turned one on since he'd known her, but Celestia did have an ultra-flat television in her sitting room and a slightly smaller one in her bedroom as well. He knew about television, about the variety of ways many people thought up what amounted to plays, created with actors or computer generated characters, but the most amazing part was the electronic devices themselves. They were capable of standing free of attachment, with those shows coming through the airwaves to fill up their screens.

Computers were just as interesting and had kept him detained longer than necessary sometimes when he should have been taking a spirit to its next stop. Over the last few decades, cell phones like the one she used but never seemed to remember to charge, as well as these other two items, had become the be-all and end-all for humans to replace the time they'd once spent working and worshiping.

Which brought him back to his purpose in securing Celestia for one of the Brotherhood. Without the special women whose lifespans were capable of traversing many generations initially and became eternal after the mating, the earth didn't stand a chance once the days of the four Blood Moons coincided with the four Holy Days foretold.

Sabin let his uncomfortable musings carry him through his shower and dressing, until he entered the small room. He was amused to see Celestia curled up in long-sleeved pajamas, watching the TV.

She was watching the evening news, her face set in consternation and concern. She glanced up at him and the tightening around her lovely eyes softened, and she held up a hand in invitation.

"I don't know why I turned this on. All I see is violence and crime, when all I really wanted to know was how the weather would be for the cookout."

He took the soft hand into his own, and every part of him felt the connection. He hadn't expected such a small touch to run so deeply through him. In all his existence, he'd never imagined how amazing having sensation would be. It was enough to make him sigh.

"There is much darkness in the world," he said, as he settled by her side. "Bad will come of it."

She nodded. "I know."

He pressed his palm against hers and curled his fingers around to touch the back of her hand. The flawless smooth skin was so white against the skin he'd been given. He took a moment to study the contrast and the fact that his long fingers cloaked nearly all that he held. Sabian allowed his gaze to slide upward, until he was again gazing into her eyes. She sighed, and he knew she was waiting for him to make some kind of move.

Sabian licked his lips in reaction and swallowed the knot in his throat. The last time he'd kissed her the earth shook, and the building broke, but they were both still here and intact. He leaned forward and that split second before their eyes slid closed and their lips melded as one, he saw the relief in those soulful eyes.

Celestia tasted of the same toothpaste she'd left for him to use, though on her it tasted even better. The minty freshness registered then he was lost in the wonder of the simple act of connection, of affection, of size and texture and movements reflecting his own. The experience took him back to his past. He was once again flying: passing planets and stars, traversing the vast universe these humans so foolishly believed they knew.

This was like finding a new galaxy, one he'd yet to know and explore. Now, the endless knowledge he'd gained since the time before time seemed underrated, and he knew he'd been arrogant in believing himself so well versed.

Celestia's free hand was on his jaw, her cool fingers awakening him from the dream he never wanted to abandon. He eased back only enough to seal the kiss, then turned his face into her palm.

She must have adjusted her body while he was so lost in the wonder of her, as she now faced him fully, one leg bent at the knee and squished between them, and one dangling over the sofa's edge. He kissed her palm once and turned to encounter her gaze again.

It nearly choked him to say the words, but they had to be said, or he was going to do something terribly stupid. "I think we should get some sleep."

It was a relief when Celestia smiled.

"I know."

He lifted the hand he'd yet to release and kissed her knuckles. "Then I will bid you goodnight."

She nodded, still smiling, and crossed over to lift the pile of bedding he hadn't noticed sitting on the small kitchen table across the room. She brought them to the couch and placed them at his side, just as she had the night before.

"Do you need help making up the couch?"

Sabian rose. "No. Thank you. I can handle it."

He knew he shouldn't have, but he pulled her to him for one last kiss. "I'll see you in the morning, beautiful."

Those stars he'd mentally passed only moments before were now sparkling from her eyes. Sabian knew sleep would be a long time coming, if at all, but he made himself yawn, just to get her safely away. Everything about her called to him. Reached for him. Demanded he forget the dangers of reaching back.

A serene smile still on her lips, Celestia nodded. "I'll see you in the morning!" She turned abruptly, her swagger light but sexy as she walked away. She threw another cheerful smile his way before she entered her room and was out of sight—and out of reach.

All he could do was stand there, filled with want and need.

****

Celestia pulled back her comforter and plopped back onto the bed. The cool sheets were exactly what she needed. Her entire body was on fire. She lay looking at the ceiling, knowing her smile was probably silly, but she didn't care. Sabastian had finally made her feel like he was as committed to what was happening between them as she.

That he'd practically sent her away, again, didn't even dampen the joy simmering in her soul. He was a gentleman clearly, since the desire to continue kissing her never left his gaze, not even when he let her go. That last glance back into his hungry eyes confirmed it for her. He wanted her just as badly as she wanted him, but his desire for more than just a physical relationship humbled her to her toes.

She'd claimed him, even while fearing doing so would cause him to desire her against his will. Or at least push him past it. She didn't really know how it all worked, but she knew once claimed by a Cavanaugh woman, men seemed to have little choice but comply. At least regarding lust. To know he was stronger of mind than the magic of her ancestors only served to increase her own desire for him. The world being what it was, and the dangers he spoke of being more frightening than he could possibly comprehend, it was comforting to know him capable of independent thought and intent. Especially since his intent was so pure.

Celestia grinned. Maybe not completely pure. He may have sent her away from him, but his body couldn't lie. She'd felt his erection when he'd held her close for that last kiss. Ah...that kiss! What a magical ride as it sent her sense tumbling into outer space, and even now played through her mind as a kaleidoscope spinning out of control. It caused her body even more agitation, but it felt so good she didn't mind.

She wasn't going to push him, them, anything, although need demanded otherwise. She actually appreciated his thinking time was required before they jumped in and took things further. Not that she would mind if he did, obviously, but just knowing he was doing what he considered the right thing, even though he wanted her so badly, made her respect him even more.

Celestia maneuvered her body so she could slide between the sheets, knowing there was little chance she'd find sleep anytime soon. She reached for the switch on her beside lamp, sending the room into darkness but for the slight door opening, where a sliver of light showed through. She knew he wouldn't come to her, his honor was too great, but she wasn't going to shut him out. If he needed or wanted her for anything, or came to decide where there was no harm, there was no foul, she wanted him to know it would be okay with her too.

Desperate for something to relax her, Celestia went over the long and exhausting day they'd shared, categorizing and compartmenting the interactions between them. So much time dealt with filth and the disgusting items Ms. Alice spent many years hoarding. But the only part to follow her into dreamland was Sabastian, once again, pulling her into his arms.

Chapter Fourteen

"So how did you make your way to West Virginia?"

Knowing he was going to have to get good at lying, Sabian allowed his greeting smile to falter, hoping his face was set in sincerity. "My mother, the woman who adopted me, died recently. I decided to fulfill a lifelong dream of finding my birthmother. It took some time since the documents were sealed. I've been all over the country for the past few years tracing one lead or another. I assume you know I finally found my grandmother, learned my birthmother had died some time ago, and then lost Granny Alice around the same time I arrived."

Logan nodded. "Yes, Sapphire told me. I'm sorry for your loss."

Sabian nodded, wondering why his eyes filled with tears, but grateful it made him look sincere and put a stop to the questions.

"Hi, Sabastian, I'm Haven. I'm Celestia's mother. I am sorry for your losses as well. Welcome to Mystic Waters."

Her smile was gentle, and her handshake ice cold. "Thank you, ma'am. It's nice to meet you."

Haven's brows pulled together and then relaxed so quickly, Sabian wondered if he'd imagined it.

"Come on over and let me introduce the rest of our clan. Or at least those of us already here."

She threw Celestia a frown. "We still haven't heard anything from Zeus. Destiny is getting worried."

The concern that crossed Celestia's features caused Sabastian to ask, "Zeus? As in the mythical God of Lightning?"

Celestia's smile was vacant. "My aunt Destiny named all her sons after Greek Gods. The two at the grill are Apollo and Heracles."

"That's interesting."

She grinned rather lopsidedly, as if suddenly aware she wasn't completely paying attention.

"All my female cousins are named for precious stones. Over there," she pointed, "is Sapphire and her husband, Nicolae. Then there," she said, pointing at a woman with equally white hair, "is Diamond. And the one holding her son is Jewell. They are what we call The Sisters White when talking about them in plural. They call my sisters and me The Sisters Hansen."

Sabian's ability to process her words became sluggish once the one she called Diamond turned his way. She smiled, nodded, and then turned back to take the baby from the redhead called Jewell.

He forced himself to look away, to focus on what Celestia said, but his equilibrium was in question, as his mind had belatedly assessed each woman in turn. Nausea was a new experience, completely unpleasant, but he choked it down, determined to get through the next few moments without revealing himself.

She is the one! The soul lost. The reason for this dilemma!

But more than recognition happened. His body writhed inside. His human heart beat wildly, until he felt it kick, and then he could barely feel it beating at all. The only thing he could think to cause his reaction was that more women with the silver blood could be near. It made sense. He had to kill Diamond as a man, but, like all angels, he had to have the ability to detect the Destined Mates if they were around.

Why hadn't he thought of that? If Celestia's blood was silver, it only made sense others in the family would have silver running though their veins too!

Celestia continued to talk, this time to her mother and father. He looked deeply into Haven's eyes, ignoring Logan all together, in an effort to determine if she was the source. He couldn't tell, had no way of knowing unless he cut into her vein, and that wasn't going to happen with so many others looking on.

It didn't really matter. She'd mated with a human and borne children years before. And she didn't have the look of eternal youth destined mates had. That was confusing. How could she have borne a child with the blood, if she herself didn't carry it?

Knowing he had no time to ponder such things, he took the opportunity to slide a glance back. It was obvious the one named Jewell was no longer a virgin since she too had borne children, so it mattered not whether she was of the silver blood. The closeness of the intimidating male who suddenly stepped to her side negated Sapphire as well. Anyone could see those two had been intimate. Diamond obviously didn't carry the silver blood, or he'd have known it when he'd tried to take her soul several human weeks earlier, when his angelic supremacies had been intact. Other than finding a way to release her soul, without alienating those he sought, she was of no interest to him or to those who expected him to deliver Celestia to them.

He glanced down at Celestia, selfishly wishing she were without the blood, disheartened there didn't seem to be more women with whom to bargain, so he might be able to keep her for his own. "And the other women?"

Surprise and something like annoyance blanketed her eyes. Sabian wondered if his question inappropriate. He didn't know. Fortunately, her features relaxed before she spoke.

"Well...my mom named the three of us with heavenly names, I guess you could say. My youngest sister, Luna, the *moon*, is walking this way with her husband Zeb, and the brunette of the family is Soleli. My mother named her Soleil, for *sun*, when we were born—we're triplets by the way, but the nurse who filled out the birth certificate mixed the letters up. My mother liked the sound of Soleli better, so she left it that way."

Sabian nodded to each as she called their names, most interested in the last. She seemed to be the only female unattached besides Celestia... He filed that away, determined to talk to her the first chance he had. He had no idea how he'd get her to bleed, but he'd have to find a way. Whether currently dating or not, if she *had* been taken by a man at any point in her life, then she was of no use to the Brotherhood. But if she *were* still pure....

Just knowing they were triplets increased the odds in his favor, making excitement rise. Claiming another with the silver blood was more than those who sent him had hoped for. Maybe there was hope he could claim Celestia as his own and still get his position back!

Feeling all eyes were on them, Sabian wondered why he felt one particular stare. He caught the frown of one of the two who looked like Celestia's mother. She shook her head slightly before turning to the Native American at her side. They moved forward together to stop in front of Celestia and him, ignoring her parents.

"I am Destiny Cavanaugh-Whitehawk. I want to know why you are here."

Sabian felt Celestia's reaction and heard her gasp, though he didn't look her way. His focus remained on the couple whose hands had joined, as they stared at him intently. He didn't like the negative feelings coming his way, or the woman's tone, but kept his features pleasant. "I came here to find family."

Celestia's mother turned to her sister with a frown but said nothing. Haven again looked him over, but the welcoming smile was gone. Until it wasn't. But this time it didn't quite ring true. She held out her hand to her daughter.

"Tom, take Sabastian on over and introduce him to the boys. Celestia, you come with me. We need some help in the kitchen."

****

She allowed her mother to pull her away, not certain what had just happened. Aunt Destiny could on occasion seem rather rude, though she only thought of herself as straightforward. Celestia would have dismissed her aunt's strange behavior if her mother weren't dragging her away from Sabastian's side. For her own mother to *demand* the help of another was completely out of character. Haven always asked, never told. And she was never rude to anyone. Well, except maybe Daddy. And those bursts were short-lived and resulted in a lot of making-up behind closed doors.

Her nerves humming, she grasped at the first thing she could think of. "Did you have to completely eliminate the snow? Do you know how strange that looks to people?"

"We were cooking out. It was in the way. And it's only here that it's all gone. I'm letting the rest of the mountain and town thaw at a more natural pace."

The realization her aunts were following them into the house increased Celestia's concern, so she let go the problem of her mother wielding her magic so blatantly. When the three matriarchs joined forces, it usually meant something was terribly out of place in the universe. Of course, they could just be planning to help prepare the food together, the norm when they all got together for a meal. But it didn't *feel* like that was what they intended.

Not wanting to borrow trouble if there was none, Celestia stopped in front of the island already filled with dishes that would complement the meats cooking outside. With such a vast array of food prepared, she was almost certain they didn't need her help at all. "What needs to be done?"

Being the most forceful of the three Cavanaugh sisters, Destiny moved behind the counter to face her. Her aunt's lips pressed tightly together, her emerald eyes filled with more anger than concern.

"Who is that man?"

Haven shook her head, looking at her sister. "Dee, don't jump on her. What did you see? What did you feel?"

Destiny inhaled and shook her head. "Nothing. I felt nothing. I saw nothing."

Celestia's insides flooded with anger as she glanced at her mother, who was frowning. She looked to her aunt Rayne, who had yet to speak. Rayne's features were neutral, her eyes interested, but she maintained her silence. Turning back to Destiny, Celestia tried to contain the irritation of knowing there was never a chance for privacy in a family with so many mystical talents. As badly as she wanted hers, that didn't mean *they* had to use theirs all the darned time!

"So, you *read* him?"

Knowing her tone was more accusatory than she'd meant it to be, Celestia awaited her aunt's answer. It was fast to come.

"I tried to, but I couldn't."

An uneasy look pasted between the sisters, but Celestia could only smile. To have her aunt's nosiness thwarted filled her with pleasure. "Then why was I dragged away, and why are we in here with you all looking so afraid?"

Instead of answering, Destiny turned her attention on Haven. "What did you feel when you touched him?"

Her mother only flashed a glance at her before addressing her sister. "Nothing. My hands were actually a little cold."

"Damn!"

Rayne's response made Celestia jump. It wasn't only

because she rarely cursed, but that she had in response to her sister's words. "What does that mean?"

Haven opened her mouth to speak, but Destiny beat her to it. "It means something is wrong with him!"

Celestia shook her head. "That isn't fair! You don't even know him."

"Do you?"

Her mother's question was rhetorical, as they knew from Sapphire she'd only just met him. But she answered anyway. "Of course I hardly know him, but he's important to me."

"You cannot claim him!"

Unable to believe her family was over reacting to Sabastian, Celestia lifted her chin, feigning innocence. "I said nothing about claiming him."

"But it's in your heart," Destiny stated, her eyes flat, her breathing strained.

"Dee, settle down. Explain what you, *we*, are thinking."

Celestia shook her head. "No, Mom. I want you all to stop this. Aunt Destiny, stop intruding in my head. Mom, I don't know why you are allowing this. You all never did this to the men my sister and cousins brought home. You welcomed them instantly! Why are you acting this way when I finally found someone *I* connect with?"

Haven shook her head, her eyes sad. "Because there is something off about him, honey. If my hands don't heat at least a little when I touch someone, it means there is no sickness in the body."

"That is a great thing, Mom!"

"No, honey, it isn't. The only time I've ever touched someone and had no reaction, that person was already dead."

Shaking her head furiously, Celestia stepped away from them. "That's ridiculous. Maybe he is just extremely healthy!"

"That would be another option," Haven said slowly. "Except that as soon as we are born, we are headed for death. There is never a moment in a human lifespan—*that I know of*—when the living body isn't touched by some sickness. It may not manifest until very old age, but it is still there, and my gift detects it."

"So you're saying Sabastian is a *zombie*?"

Rayne moved closer, and Celestia hoped for a more reasonable explanation. Of the three matriarchs, she was the more studious and logical.

"Celestia, honey, you must calm down. We aren't here to take what you want from you, but to make sure you aren't facing danger. Please, let them explain what they are sensing."

She nodded. "Okay. Aunt Destiny, what does it mean that you can't read him?"

After a long pause, Destiny closed her eyes and bowed her head. "I'm not entirely sure, but I think it means he doesn't have a soul."

They were wrong! She knew they were. "I don't believe that. I have seen him react to the pain of losing his grandmother only hours before he could have met her. Of learning his mother was dead before he found her. He has a soul! And he isn't dead! So you had all better find out why your gifts aren't working on him! Consult your precious diaries!"

"Celestia!"

Ignoring her mother's distress, Celestia looked at each one in turn, filled with an anger she'd never before experienced. "I have heard enough! This little talk is over."

She fled from the kitchen, determined to prove them wrong. She had no idea how she would, but she would. She returned to the front porch only to find the others silently watching the door. Afraid their voices had carried, she sought Sabastian, only to find him deep in conversation with Soleli. She flew to him and took his hand to drag him away. As angry as she was, the last thing she needed was for him to be flirting with her sister.

"What's wrong?"

Celestia shook her head, relieved at least he hadn't heard the ridiculous conversation. "Nothing. I just wanted to take a walk. Come with me. Let me show you the beauty of the mountain."

He allowed her to lead them to the tree line in silence but stopped her when they were out of sight of the others. "Celestia, why are you angry?"

Knowing there was no way she could explain her family had mystical gifts that had condemned him, she took a deep breath and smiled. "Nothing. My mother and aunts were giving me the third degree over you. I wasn't in the mood to be questioned."

"The third degree?"

"Yes. They wanted to know everything about you, and I don't know everything about you. I decided we needed to take a walk and get to know each other better."

Sabastian frowned. "They don't like me?"

Not about to let him worry over that, she shook her head and lied outright. "Of course they will, once they get to know you. It's more about my being attracted to you that worries them. It happens every time a new man or woman comes into our lives."

Sabastian nodded. "That's a relief. I need for them to like me."

Delighted he cared enough for her to want her family's approval, Celestia walked a little faster. She needed to get as far as possible from the large cabin to find privacy and calm down. She knew Sapphire and Nicolae could hear for miles if they so desired, but she knew they never intruded unless they had sound reason to do so.

Hopefully her mother and aunts hadn't told them there

was reason.

"I want to get to know you, Sabastian, but I want to show you some things first. I can't imagine there is another place on earth as beautiful as this mountain, though people probably always feel that's true of the place they call home."

"It is by far a favorite of The Creator."

Celestia stumbled and turned to him. "What?"

Sabastian looked slightly appalled for only seconds, making her wonder if she'd misinterpreted the flash of expression. He grinned suddenly, taking her breath.

"I meant it is very beautiful. As are you."

Pleasure warmed her skin. "As are you, as well."

He stared at her, and Celestia had to fight to maintain eye contact. It was suddenly difficult to look upon him for too long for some reason, and she feared her aunt had sent a spell to make it so. Her eyes closed of their own volition, forcing her to struggle to open them several times before she gave up and looked around them. Fury filled her, and she knew she was going to be totally rude to her aunt once they returned to the cabin.

"Are you unwell?"

Truly mortified, she shook her head and cleared her throat. "No. I'm fine." Knowing she'd have to say something or continue to struggle with discomfort, Celestia spouted, "It's just I'm so very attracted to you, and I don't know what to do about it."

The touch of his hand taking hers made her flinch. Her mother and aunts were dead wrong about him. There was plenty of heat coming from his palm.

"I desire to be with you also."

She peered at him for as long as she could and then pulled him forward so her hug prevented having to look at him. Irritation found its way back. Her family was supposed to be there in her time of need! Not make her look like an idiot!

But what if they were right? What if he wasn't who and what he appeared to be? It was stupid to give their words credence, but they never seemed to be wrong. Celestia took a deep breath and blew it out.

"I need to ask you a question that isn't going to make any sense at all."

Sabastian's chest raised and lowered, and his heartbeat belied their words.

"What do you wish to know?"

Licking her lips, Celestia gathered her courage. "Is there anything about you that isn't human?"

****

Sabian remained perfectly still. At least most of him did. Her warm body arched slightly as it aligned with his. Instead of awaiting his answer, she raised her face to him with eyes closed, as if expecting a kiss.

He leaned down and gently took her lips before straightening.

"Forget I said that."

Her high firm breasts pushed into his ribcage, teasing the abdominal muscles he'd never before noticed. The softness of her stomach pushed against the rise of his human genitals, creating those confusing sensations that made him want to thrust forward, making it hard for him to remember her question. His gaze sought hers, but her eyes remained closed, so he had no choice but to focus on her slightly parted plump lips again. He found himself licking his own as a hunger he didn't expect, given the question he now remembered, filled him. A crack of thunder in the nearly cloudless sky made him jerk and step back. The look of distress and anger in her eyes startled him even more.

"Motherfuc—!"

Sabian moved forward quickly, needing to stop Celestia before she finished the curse. He had no desire to be struck by lightning, but more importantly, he couldn't allow harm to come to her. He swooped her up and took her open mouth only to silence her, but she stilled in his arms, and her astonished eyes slowly slid closed.

The taste of her stopped him from an immediate retreat, the texture of her lips and tongue as it glided over his, took his breath. He allowed each sensation to fill him and shook with a want that only built each time he touched her. Another rumble filled the air, but this time it was more gentle and nonthreatening, so he continued his exploration and allowed her the same. Though he felt no immediate threat from the heavens, he pulled back slowly anyway, afraid the emotions and physical reactions swamping him would lead to places he had no business going. It took effort, but he finally settled her back upon the ground.

They stood there silently for what seemed endless moments, but the concept of human time was still too new for Sabian to know just how long. He swallowed several times, alternately worried and relieved he had no idea what those who watched him and Celestia thought. He had no doubt about being watched, though. He took one last deep breath and sent an apology skyward, hoping talking to the Master directly helped his case.

Of course, there was no answer. He hadn't expected one. He had sinned, and The Creator did not look upon sin.

"I need to take you back to your family."

Celestia shook her head. "I don't wish to go back just yet."

"You said the celebration is in your honor," he reminded her, determined to get away from her until he could analyze the feelings flooding him.

Looking defeated, she nodded. "I'd somehow forgotten that. I guess we do have to."

Sabian frowned at her, wondering what had changed.

She'd been eager to join her family before they'd arrived, and now she wasn't. Had someone said something negative about him? Did Sapphire have time to look into his past, only to find it didn't exist? He bit his bottom lip, determined to find out.

"Yes, let's get on back."

****

Celestia didn't know what to think. About *anything*.

Sabastian expressed delight one moment about being with her, had kissed her until her toes curled, then retreated with a haste that left her befuddled. She practically had to run to keep up with his long determined strides as they walked back to the clearing that lead to Uncle Tom and Aunt Destiny's cabin. Fortunately, when they broke the tree line, everyone seemed to be going about their business as usual.

The long tables always used to holding the mountain of foods prepared for their gatherings were in place, and were being covered as her cousins and their men brought bowls and containers from inside the house. The two Whitehawk cousins present were taking the meat from the grill and placing everything from pork ribs to whole chickens into large baking dishes to set at the head of the table, closest to the plates and silverware. Sapphire's little black and white Shih Tzu was messing up her latest grooming by rolling around in a patch of dirt with Uncle Garrison's new bloodhound puppy. Aunt Destiny's big black cat licked at her paws while watching them with disdain. Since her father and the uncles were nowhere in sight, she just imagined they were up to something that involved her graduation gift. There was *always* a gift involved when any of their children reached a milestone in life.

Her mother and the aunts filed out the front door without babies in their arms, which meant the little jewels were sound asleep inside. Haven glanced her way and said something to her sisters before heading in their direction. Celestia stiffened, afraid her mother would continue with her concerns in front of Sabastian. It was the last thing she needed and would be the last straw.

"You made it back just in time to eat," Haven said, her eyes reflecting gentle concern.

Relieved they weren't to be verbally attacked, Celestia relaxed. "It smells good."

Haven nodded and looked up at Sabastian. "I hope you're hungry, we have pork, beef, and chicken. Enough to feed an army."

Sabastian smiled at her. "I find my stomach does require nourishment, thank you."

Celestia caught her mother's quick blink, knowing it resulted from the phrasing of his response. She glanced up to him, seeing nothing but pleasure in his eyes and a slight grin on his lips. Deciding she wasn't going to let her families' imaginations ruin the day for her, Celestia moved forward, ready to get the celebration started. So it could end. She was no longer in the mood to be around her family, knowing Aunt Destiny was more likely than not, going to start trouble. It was obvious her aunt felt Sabastian some kind of threat.

"Let's eat," Celestia said, taking his hand before thinking. She made her way to the table, knowing her family would require her, as guest of honor, to go first. And sure enough, as soon as she and Sabastian were making their plates, everyone fell into lines on either side of the tables behind them.

It was such a relief that there was lots of chatter. Everyone picked and chose their favorite foods. Inconsequential words passed back and forth between her cousins and Sabastian, and he seemed to be comfortable with them all. Until Aunt Destiny intercepted him at the drink table and asked what he preferred.

Sabastian stared at the array of soft drinks, pitchers of tea, and the open cooler filled with beer, bottled waters and ice. He glanced up to Destiny, his eyes filled with indecision. "You pick for me."

Celestia glanced at her aunt, only to find her staring hard into Sabastian's eyes. A chill went down her spine, and she swallowed against the knot in her throat. It was clear Destiny was trying to read him again, and the frustration in her eyes made it clear she wasn't getting anywhere.

Stepping around him, Celestia reached for a water but ended up lifting a beer. She frowned, having no idea if he drank alcohol or not, but she wasn't about to return it. She handed it to him and took his arm to lead him to the many vacant chairs circling the cold fire pit.

To her relief her family seemed to understand now was not the time to make things more difficult, and talk turned to celebrating Dia's pregnancy, and the subsequent return of her memories that led to it.

"She's pregnant?"

The pasty hue of Sabastian's skin sent disappointment down Celestia's spine. If the man she'd claimed didn't want children, she'd have to convince him otherwise. She wanted lots and lots and lots.

She only nodded and took a bite of potato salad as talked turned to the sad news involving Gavin and his son. She listened, wishing she'd known her California cousin better, and could help in some way to ease the distress he and his child were experiencing.

The sound of her cell phone broke up the chatter, and she pulled it from the light jacket she wore. The number was unknown to her, but that was to be expected. With the exception of Zeus and Luna, anyone on her contact list was present.

The conversation was quick and filled her with relief.

She had her out. "I need to get back to the clinic. A dog's been hit by a truck, and the man is there waiting for me now." She stood, and Sabastian followed suit.

He smiled. "Thank you for having me. I look forward to seeing you again."

Celestia noticed most of her family made the appropriate responses but Destiny said nothing at all. She swallowed, determined to ignore her sourpuss aunt.

Chapter Fifteen

After the weird family gathering the day before, the surgery she'd had to perform to removed the dog's mangled leg at the hip joint and the time spent comforting the man who had hit him, Celestia didn't feel much like cleaning out an old lady's nasty house today. But a promise was a promise, and she knew it was dishonest to tell herself she didn't want to spend the day with Sabastian again, even though she'd been up all night worrying over the matriarchs' reaction to him.

Celestia dressed in what were now her least favorite clothes. Though they laundered well enough, she would throw them out once her help with the cleaning was no longer required. She was tired and, as much as she'd fought it, was now convinced she needed to proceed with caution. There were no illusions about her experience with men, since she had so little. And she knew there were those who sought their kind to expose and destroy them, which wasn't something to ignore.

Celestia clamped her teeth together so hard, pain hit her temples. She refused to believe Sabastian capable of such deception, no matter her family's concerns.

The worrisome thoughts carried her to the window facing his house.

It was a little breath-stealing to find a muscle-bound Sabastian shirtless, while pushing an old lawn mower through the front yard's tall brown grass. The realization that *all* the snow was now gone was as startling as her forgetting just how beautiful his body was. She licked her lips, certain she had more sense than to let his ridiculously gorgeous form sway her into forgetting all the lectures she'd given herself throughout the night.

Sabastian must have sensed he was being watched. He stopped pushing the mower, glanced around, then turned her way and looked up with a smile and a wave. She feared she really was in over her head if he turned out to be something other than the man she had come to know.

The sound of the mower whined to a halt. Celestia sucked in a breath and pasted a smile on her lips, determined to learn all she could. She waved back and turned to hurry out of the house and across the parking lot. She *had* to believe Sabastian was just what he seemed. A little out of place in Mystic Waters, somewhat lost after having searched for family only to lose them to death. Nothing more and nothing less.

She approached him with a smile. "Good morning. You're up early."

The pleasure in his eyes when he looked her over sent tingles down her spine.

"Good morning. I thought I'd try to clean up the yard before you got here. It seemed the easiest task to accomplish, especially since all that snow practically disappeared, and the ground is actually dry. I didn't expect it to melt so quickly.

There was nothing Celestia could say. Her mother's intent was good, but she sometimes—*often really*—used her magic without thought of consequences. Since Haven Cavanaugh-Hansen didn't have a deceitful bone in her body, she never took the time to process doing things in an underhanded way. She just did what she thought best at any given moment and let the chips fall where they may. Great, usually. But this time too many people, and Sabastian in particular as a newcomer to the area, would find it odd, the snow practically *poofed* away.

"I looked over the house when I got up earlier. We've

actually accomplished a lot. By the end of the day, I'm hopeful the last of the trash will be out, and I can start making plans about the structure. All the carpet has to go and the linoleum, obviously. With the exception of that corner in the kitchen by the sink, I think the drywall is okay. Scraping and painting throughout mostly."

He smiled at her. "I can take it from here. You've already done more than enough."

Celestia was more than happy to be done with the nasty work, but it meant she'd have time on her hands to worry over who he really was. Being near him for only these few minutes had pushed those concerns away. Now she'd have to confront them and spend time on the computer trying to investigate him.

She wasn't ready to go there yet, and angry Aunt Destiny had filled her mind with these darts of mistrust. "Okay. But I'm ready and still don't have any patients— which is really starting to worry me. I could stand to keep my hands busy. What if I help for just a little while? It will get you that much further along."

Sabastian wiped sweat from his brow and examined his moist palm as if sweating was something odd. Celestia looked away, even more irritated, knowing she would have made nothing of it if these doubts weren't clouding her thoughts. Since the snow had melted, or *disappeared* as was really the case, the morning held only the slight chill of early fall. Exerting himself to cut down the tall grass could account for sweating, as well as shirtlessness.

But, she had to acknowledge, not that odd look in his eyes.

"If you want, sure. I just knew yesterday was a long day for you, and you look a little tired this morning. I didn't want to ask more of you. You've already done so much."

Celestia felt at odds. Although his words seemed sincere, the impression he was pushing her away settled in.

She hoped she was reading him wrong, but she had no idea if that was the case or not.

"Come on, then. I can show you where we are. I awoke early and hit it, so there really isn't all that much left to do."

She nodded and preceded him to the back door. When they entered, she was amazed at the difference. He must not have slept at all. Nearly all the clutter left from the day before yesterday, which she'd expected to help him with, was already handled.

"Better?"

She nodded. "Yes, it is." She smiled at him, but he didn't smile back. Hers fell, and she looked away.

"What are you thinking?"

Celestia glanced back up and saw that spark of purely male interest. He was confusing her this morning. Welcoming, then businesslike, then cool, and then this. She wanted to move closer, test the waters, to see if the passion and care were still there on his part.

She held back, determined to take things slow, especially since she could put her aunt's questions to rest completely, and now, her own. "I was wondering about your heritage."

His eyes flashed, but she couldn't decipher his reaction.

"I'm Alaskan."

He'd already said that, when his memories had started returning. "I know. I meant further back. Where did your people originate from?"

After a slight pause, he shrugged. "I don't know exactly. I told you, I was adopted and there's no one left here to ask."

"Oh, that's right! Maybe we can get information on Ms. Alice and trace her history. I'm good at researching, and the Internet is a fabulous place to find out all kinds of things about people. Have you run across a family Bible? I never saw one, but you've done more since I was last here."

Sabastian remained completely still. "Why do you care so much?"

Celestia felt slapped by his tone. "I'm sorry. I didn't mean to intrude." She turned away, not sure what to do, but immediately felt his hand on her shoulder, turning her back to face him.

"I'm sorry. That sounded harsher than I meant it to be."

He looked into her eyes until Celestia had to fight to maintain eye contact. It baffled her why that was. She shrugged. "I'm sorry, really. I think in your place I would want to know, but it was wrong of me to put that on you."

She hated that her aunt's suspicions had settled in. Everything he did or said now was suspect. It wasn't fair to either of them. "Let's just get to work and get to know the people we are. It doesn't matter where we came from."

He seemed to relax, but that only made her more curious. Even though they were smiling at each other, she knew she had just lied to him. The first chance she got, she was going to start digging. And she didn't mean in the old lady's trash.

****

Sabian took a relieved breath. The last thing he needed was anyone uncovering the lack of his existence. He knew enough about the current generation to know they had access to just about everyone and everything, if they were willing to put out time and, in some cases, money to uncover it. He had wondered often over the past few decades if humans realized how dangerous their curiosity was. His situation aside, their need to discover the origins and workings of their universe, rather than live in faith, was what would lead to their extinction. Only *The Creator* was meant to know all, and *He* would never allow that to change.

Knowing he was a prime example of what disasters could befall those delving into the forbidden, Sabian took a step back. He had no choice but to ignore the physical attraction or the emotional ones he felt for the beautiful woman standing before him. Now that he'd found the one whose soul had to be returned to Heaven, he had to get the ball rolling. Wishful thinking that he could keep Celestia for himself if her sister, Soleli, was also one of The Chosen, was what had kept him up all night. That's all it was: *wishful thinking*. If he'd been fortunate enough to find two of the women they sought, then both would soon be used for the greater purpose.

"Let's get some things done before the day gets too warm."

Celestia nodded, and he wished again for his lost angelic supremacies so he could determine if her expression was from hurt or confusion. He wasn't sure which, but he was certain their mutual attraction would only lead to trouble if he didn't finish this thing soon. He had no choice but to remain aloof to a degree. But if too distant, it would probably kill his chances of success when he had to get her to agree to go with him, after taking her cousin's life.

It was quite a dilemma, and now that his goals were attainable, it only seemed bigger.

"I want to ask you something first."

Sabian nodded, as a tingling of unease settled in the center of his body. "Yes?"

She bit her lip and then focused on him with squinting eyes. "I asked you a question back at my aunt and uncle's place, but you never answered."

Deciding he had no choice but to make light of it, he grinned. "You wanted to know if I'm human or not."

She nodded, surprise in her eyes. "Well, *yes*."

He laughed, and hoped it rang true. "That's a strange

question to ask someone. If I'm not, what in the world would I be?"

The relief in her eyes accompanied a self-depreciating grin. "What indeed."

Thinking he'd dodged that bullet, Sabian reached for her hand and heard her gasp of pleasure. A slam of desire to pull her closer was his immediate reaction, but it wasn't something he was willing to indulge. He had to remain resolved. He'd only meant to get them going so they could work and talk about her and *her* family. He needed information so he could make a plan of action that would get him out of this mess. But the awareness of their physically connection, each time they made contact, was clearly going to be a problem. And he was seriously afraid it had been done to him on purpose.

Knowing it too dangerous to question if that were true or not, he released her hand and sighed. "Let's finish up the kitchen, and maybe even scrub the bathrooms today. I think those two areas are what is causing the worst of the odor."

Celestia's face reflected her distaste, but she nodded. "Okay. Do I need a hazmat suit?"

It took him several seconds to realize she was joking, *maybe*. He shook his head. "I'll do the nasty stuff if you'll just start bagging up everything in the bathrooms we can get rid of."

She nodded, her relief obvious.

"That works for me. I'll throw everything away, unless it looks like something you might want to keep. I'll set those things aside and you can decide what you want to do with them."

"I doubt there is anything I'd keep. Just bag everything up, and let's get this done." *All of it!*

"What about the yard? I stopped you from finishing it."

The yard didn't matter any more than the house did. He was only doing these things to retain legitimacy in her eyes. Once he'd taken a life, and possibly delivered two others into eternal bondage, he'd never see the place again.

Half an hour later, Sabian decided bleach was definitely his new best friend.

After Celestia bagged the thousands of items stored under the vanity's sink and all around the floor, she left him to the small mold-infested room. It wasn't long before he'd removed the last of the black mold from around the waterline behind the toilet and poured another half-gallon of bleach into the toilet's bowl. As he stood back to survey his work, he wondered how anyone could live as Ms. Alice had. He'd seen the way hoarders lived when he was himself, but experiencing it as a human was completely different.

"Look what I found."

Startled, Sabian flinched. Celestia was holding what seemed to be a heavy little box. She held it by the handle, as well as supported the base, before she sat it at his feet.

"It's a lock box. Maybe it has papers in it that will give you more information on your family."

Sabian tried not to let his irritation show. Her obsession with finding his roots would have been great if he was who she believed him to be. As it was, it only complicated things. He eyed her, wishing she weren't so beautiful, so sweet, so everything he never knew he'd want, even when a mess. The disheveled hair, the stains on her shirt, and the smudge of what looked to be ash on her cheek should have taken something away...but didn't. She was a piece of art with a heart of gold. No one else would have jumped in to help a complete stranger clear out and clean up what had to be one of the nastiest places on the entire planet.

And he was here to steal her life, possibly her sister's, and kill and take the soul of another she loved.

For the first time since his creation, Sabian wanted to throw off the shackles of angelic obligation. Wondering what it would be like to look at her with the purpose of pursuing her, he indulged in the vision of taking her into his arms and kissing her until the stars fell from the sky. Of taking that body and worshiping every inch of it. But to do so would be a final act of defiance he couldn't afford. Not only would he not get to keep her, he would be nothing.

He glanced at the box, then up at the look of excitement in her eyes. "Thanks. I'll check it out later. I need to get cleaned up. I feel like germs are crawling all over me."

Her smile brightened. "That sounds great. Me too. I've loaded the bags I filled into the truck. Why don't we both wash up, and we can drop them off at the dump on our way back from getting some lunch? I haven't had time to grocery shop, and there is a fairly new restaurant in town I love."

Sabian nodded. He hadn't thought of food until she mentioned it, but with all the nasty things he'd had to deal with, he wasn't surprised. Only now, his midsection felt hollow. "Sounds good to me. You go first. I'll finish the patch of grass I was working on and be in soon. About half an hour?"

She nodded, smiling. "That sounds perfect."

Sabian watched her go and listened for the outer door closing before looking down at the box at his feet. He needed the opportunity to examine the contents without Celestia around. If there were family records in there, they might include something to risk his assumed position as a member of Ms. Alice's family.

He squatted and examined the box, relieved to see the little lock attached would be simple to break, if it didn't break the little box while he tried getting it off. Carrying it to the kitchen, Sabian placed it on the now clean tabletop, and used the screwdriver to twist the lock off. Sure enough, the short nails holding the latch gave first, but he didn't care. As soon as he examined the contents, and disposed of any needed, he'd just tell her curiosity got the better of him.

There was the deed to the house, several envelopes aged with time, old black and white pictures he took a few minutes to study, a larger yellow envelope filled with hundred dollar bills and at the bottom—a will.

Why he felt like a thief, Sabian didn't know. But he did. Since it was the least of the sins he would commit in the coming days, he pushed the guilt away, and unfolded the will. The contents were simple enough and held no threat. Ms. Alice left everything to her daughter, and in the event of her dying first, if her child could be found, to him.

There was no relief. He wouldn't benefit from this person's legacy. Before long others would come into this house, and he'd leave the box for them to find. If the actual grandchild ever showed up, he'd have something with which to connect him to his birth family. If he never came, eventually, someone else would do something with it all. It was no concern of his.

Except it felt as if it was.

Sometime in the cleaning, the caring, and in the planning with Celestia regarding the house, it started to be his home. Sabian shook his head at how being human had turned him foolish, but he couldn't completely shake off his wish it were true.

****

The food smelled wonderful as steam rose up to tease her nostrils, but Celestia couldn't eat. As much as she'd tried to cast away her doubts, Sabastian not wanting to look into that box, after claiming he'd spent a great deal of time searching for his birth family, had gnawed at her through showering, dressing, waiting for him to get cleaned up and ready, and their trip here.

He should have been excited at the possibility of discovering what was in the box. It should have mattered more than dirty hands and a hungry stomach. His somber then cheerful moods, after he'd returned to the house and never looked directly at her when he spoke, only served to tighten the knots in her already upset stomach.

She lifted the fork to her mouth and set it back down without taking the bite. Not looking up, she forced herself to speak. "We need to talk."

Celestia could see Sabastian's fork settling on his plate with her peripheral vision. She lifted her head and met his eyes. There was tension in them, and hers increased.

"Sure. What do you want to talk about?"

How did she start? Did she tell him of her family's suspicions? Tell him about how they came to have them? She blew out a breath. "I need to understand why you didn't want to look in the box."

Sabastian's lips quivered. He swallowed. Then he shrugged. "I did, after all. Curiosity got the better of me."

Why that made her exhale so strongly, Celestia didn't want to know. "You didn't say anything."

Sabastian looked away briefly, then back. "I didn't think about it. The expected things are there. House deed, will, some money, pictures. She left the house to her daughter and then to the grandchild she never knew. So I guess that makes everything easier for me."

Celestia nodded, but the reassurance wasn't there. Maybe because he wasn't excited. Just knowing he had something of his family's....

What was she doing? Celestia wondered, exasperated. It wasn't fair of her to dictate how he was to respond. If anything, his somber attitude was more respectful to those he lost. She forced a smile. "That's great. I'm glad for you."

"What's going on?"

His tightly spoken question caught her off guard.

"What do you mean?"

Sabastian settled back in his seat. "Ever since we went to your family's place you've been different. What is going on?"

She studied his eyes, knowing she had to give some explanation but feared being honest. She had to protect her family, even if she was willing to risk herself. "They are concerned for me. You popped up out of nowhere, under the strangest of circumstances. They think I've fallen too hard for you, too fast."

All of it was truth and the most she could give him until she was more sure of his feelings and who he really was. He sighed deeply, and she almost believed in relief. But why would that ease his worry? He'd plainly stated he wanted them to like him.

"How far have you fallen?"

The question wasn't what she expected, but she knew she had to be completely honest about this. She'd claimed him. If giving him her heart on a platter was all that concerned him, then she was more than willing to do so. "I'm in love with you."

He stared at her, then his face crumbled, and he quickly rose and walked out of the restaurant. Celestia closed her mouth, since her jaw had fallen open at his surprising reaction to her declaration of love. She quickly dug out enough cash to cover their uneaten meals and hurried to catch up with him.

Sabastian stood beside her truck, both hands clasping the bed, is head down. She approached slowly, stopping at his side. There were questions, but she didn't know what to ask.

He turned her way, his eyes filled with anguish. "I have to kill Diamond."

Chapter Sixteen

Celestia stumbled back, her mind reeling, her stomach threatening to revolt. She shook her head, determined to release the horror blocking her ability to think. Tears filled her eyes and streamed down her face, as denial choked her throat closed.

He advanced on her quickly, making her scurry back further. The determined look on his face and his gaining strides sent her into panic mode. She turned abruptly, determined to get as far from him as she could, but his large hand landed on her shoulder and spun her back around before he pulled her into a tight hug.

"Let me go!" she screamed, only to find herself lifted into his arms. He had them back at the truck in an instant. He lowered her so she could stand but held her tightly as he thrust his hand into her purse.

"Listen to me! You have to calm down. I will explain everything, if I don't disappear first! Celestia, stop it!" he nearly shouted. "We may not have much time!"

His words made no sense! "What are you talking about? How can tell me you want to kill my cousin and then expect me to listen to another word coming out of your deceitful mouth?"

Sabastian pulled the keys from her purse and pressed the button, the loud click indicating he'd unlocked the doors. He opened the driver's door and lifted her, thrusting her across the seat, ignoring her attempt to push him back out as he followed. She wiggled her way to the other side and reached for the handle, but he hit the lock, and the darned child safety must have been on. Her door wouldn't unlock without him releasing it.

She turned on him and swatted, her attempts feeble. She'd never hit another soul in her life and wasn't built to fight. Sabastian grabbed her hands and fisted both in one of his, before clamping down on her wrists. He held her with his right hand, contorting to start the truck with his left, and blew out a breath as he started threw it into drive.

"Stop it!" Sabastian shouted, when she continued to struggle. "You're going to get killed. I've never driven before!"

She knew he had no driver's license since he'd entered her life with nothing, but his statement made no sense. There was no way he'd lived all this time and hadn't learned to drive. Unless he was an alien—or zombie, like her aunt believed!

Celestia made herself go completely still, which caused him to look over at her briefly before he turned back to the road. She did as well, surprised to see they were heading out of town, not back to the clinic or his house, and her fear increased. And then relief swamped her. If he thought to go back and find Dia at Tom and Destiny's cabin, he'd be out of luck. Dia was more than likely holed-up with Ryan at her own place, safely out of his reach.

"Why are you doing this?" she asked tightly, barely able to talk to him now.

"If you promise to sit still I'll let your wrists go. I need my hands free to keep from killing you once we get to the mountain roads."

That was the second time he'd said she would be the one to die if she didn't let him drive. She nodded when he looked her way, then she scooted over only enough to put her seatbelt on. She could see he almost reached for her again but moved his free hand to grasp the steering wheel when he realized she was cooperating.

"You won't die too?"

Sabastian didn't look her way, but held tightly to the steering wheel as he shook his head. "Not like you think."

Destiny was right!

"What does that mean?"

"It means I will not exist."

Chills flew up her spine and raised the hairs over her body. "What are you?"

He leaned forward and looked up into the sky before leaning back and taking a deep breath. "I can't tell you. Not yet."

Not a zombie! An alien! From another planet! "Why would you kill my cousin? She's done nothing to you."

Even in profile, she could tell Sabastian was struggling to find a way to answer. She crossed her arms and turned to face forward as well. Since they'd rounded a good part of Mystic Lake, and the mountain loomed before them, Celestia tried to come to grips with what was happening. She couldn't freak out. After all, her family members were oddities according to most of the rest of the world. She had to find a way to contact her mother and the others, but she'd never had that ability without using her phone.

Aunt Destiny was her only hope. If her aunt was still talking to her. Destiny, with her abilities, clearly knew just what Celestia thought about her when they'd left the cookout. Those abilities could reach out to her again, if Destiny chose to listen.

Celestia closed her eyes and concentrated on the face so like her own mothers. The three matriarchs were still identical in every way, but she could choose the one she wanted, if her aunt was willing to receive her message. *I need you! I need my mom! And I think we'll need Aunt Rayne too! Please. I'm sorry! You were right! I think I'm being brought to either your place or to Mom and Dad's. Find me. And find Dia! Get her as far from the mountain as you can!*

"What are you doing?"

Celestia jumped and turned her head to find him alternately watching her and the road. "I'm trying to figure out what's really going on."

He nodded and continued driving. "I don't know how much of it I can explain. And I'm trying to find a way out. I need you to trust me. Or at least trust I don't want to hurt you."

"*Trust you?* You've been lying to me since we met! You want to kill my cousin! How the hell am I supposed to *trust* you?"

Tears flooded her eyes, and she was angry for allowing them to develop, even though she had no control over it. She sniffed hard, determined to keep herself together. Falling apart wasn't an option whether her aunt heard her or not. She had to find a way to get away from him, and she had to make sure Dia did too. There was no way she would allow her cousin to be murdered. Not by anyone, and certainly not by the man she'd mistakenly tied her heart to.

"Because I have no choice! I'm not even supposed to be telling you all this. But I've fallen in love with you too, and I'm doing the only thing I can now. I just hope I can do it before I'm taken."

"You mean beamed up to the Mother Ship?"

Her snide comment didn't get the expected reaction. Sabastian actually had the audacity to chuckle, making her want to undo her seatbelt and attack him again.

"Something like that," he said, the smile still hovering on his lips.

"There is nothing funny about this!"

His smile disappeared instantly. "No. There isn't."

"Just let me go. Leave my cousin alone! Go back to wherever it is you came from!"

Sabastian slowed down when he approached Dead Man's Curve, not bothering to look her way. "I can't. The choice isn't mine."

"You already said that! But it is! There is always a choice!" Impotent fury accompanied her words. They seemed to have no effect on him. She shook her head, knowing her greatest hope lay just beyond the curve, if her aunt Destiny had contacted her mother and Rayne. If she hadn't received the message, Celestia knew there was only one thing left to do.

The gun in the glove box was her father's idea, and one she'd never expected to consider needing. She knew she couldn't pull it on him while he drove, or she'd end up dead as well. Her only hope was, once they stopped, he'd get out of the truck and expect her to do the same from her side. Killing him was the only thing she could think of to end this horror. As abhorrent as it was, she'd have to do whatever she had to do to protect Dia.

"Sometimes, even if you're willing to give up everything, the decision is not yours to make."

Celestia blew out a breath. What did that mean? If she eliminated him as a threat to her cousin, others would come and take Dia's life anyway?

"Why?"

"I told you, I can't say. Please, I'm trying to work this all out myself. I need you to give me your trust. No matter what happens, it's the only hope we have."

Celestia bit her bottom lip, torn in so many directions. Could she believe in him when her cousin's life was at stake? She wanted to, even with all this, she so desperately wanted to.

She could blame it on having claimed him. She wouldn't have done so if he weren't the only man meant for her. Alien or not, she was connected to him with an invisible chain. That tether meant everything or nothing. As much as her mind said to reject him, her heart wouldn't allow her to do so. "If you kill Dia, you end my life as well."

"If I don't, all of our lives are over, unless…."

Celestia sat up straighter. "Unless, what?"

Sabastian shook his head. "Unless there is mercy."

****

There was a sense of relief when Sabastian slowed and then turned into the long driveway leading to Tom and Destiny's property. And an even greater one when they passed the last of the forested drive and her mother and two aunts were standing in front of the large cabin. Celestia's eyes filled as excitement and dread clutched her chest. Her heart pounded with such power she was afraid the resulting black spots swirling in her eyes meant she was about to pass out. She gripped the door handle hard as she fought to stay conscious, hoping Sabastian would release the lock as soon as they stopped. He did, and she flew out of the cab and ran to the warmth and security of her mother's arms.

Celestia turned to watch as Sabastian slowly climbed from the cab, his face set in stone, his eyes determined. He approached them, and all three matriarchs raised a hand, palm out, to stop him. He did stop as was expected, but only for a second.

She gasped, as well as the women standing around her, since none before had ever overcome the power of *The Three*. When Sabastian was only feet before them, he stopped on his own.

"You have no place here, alien!" Destiny said, her voice echoing with the power of her fury.

Sabastian's lips pressed together as his gaze turned to her. "You are right. I don't. But I had no choice in coming."

There was pregnant pause as they stared at each other, and Celestia felt Haven's attempt to pull her back. She licked her lips and stood her ground in spite of her mother's efforts. Now that the time had come to hand him over to those with great power, she couldn't do so without her heart ripping in two.

"You better have a choice in leaving on your own, or we will do it for you."

He looked from one woman to the next, his gaze sorrowful when landing on Celestia. "Where is Dia?"

Rayne stepped forward, anger radiating from her visage. "You will not have my daughter! I will kill you first!"

His body jerked, and to Celestia's surprise, his appearance began to change. He grew taller, his lean muscles increased in size and depth, and his dark hair lightened until it was a golden blond, and curled tightly against his head. His clothing was replaced with the same outfit of the man who had scared her at the clinic. No wonder he hadn't wanted her to report it! It was another of his kind!

Gasps again passed the lips of the four women, and to her amazement, they backed away, Haven pulling her as well.

Rayne jerked Celestia behind them before she knew what was happening, and *The Cavanaugh Three* clasped hands.

"You!" Rayne said, her voice shaking with fury, "You are that man my daughters saw in Europe a couple of years ago! They all three were in different countries but saw you at the same time!"

Destiny turned to her sister, her eyes filled with fear. "Right before Jewell was thrown back into Ancient Egypt! I remember!" She turned to Sabastian, equal wrath in her words. "You have been stalking our family for years! *Why?* What do you want?"

Sabastian shook his head as he looked at his larger arms and hands. Confusion filled his eyes, but his words were strong when he again looked up and at them all.

"It was not I. I am restored and am again Sabian,

former Reaper of the Dead. That was another, probably the one looking for Celestia. Perhaps for Luna and Soleli as well."

Celestia fought shock at his altered appearance, but her mother's trembling was her first concern. She broke the connection of Haven's handholding with Rayne to join hands with each. Together the power of *The Three* was unstoppable, or it had been, but this was her family too, and she would not be a coward. "Why? Why look for my sisters and me? And what does Dia have to do with any of it?"

Sabian closed his eyes briefly then opened them. "If I am not taken before the telling, then I will explain. But you must know. Now, no matter what happens, Diamond must die, and Celestia, and possibly her younger sister Soleli, will be taken. Luna, the youngest, is no longer of value."

"Taken *where*?" Haven, Destiny, and Rayne demanded at the same time.

Sabian glanced up and seemed to be waiting. They all did as well. Eventually his head lowered, and he was again looking from one of them to the next. "Heaven."

Denial and fear had each woman shaking her head. They were dealing with an angel and powers greater than their own. It was Celestia who spoke past the tightness of her throat. "*Why?*"

"I can only explain it fully if I start before man was on the earth."

At their nods, Sabian lowered his head and then slowly lifted it as the curve of large white wings appeared over his shoulders, spreading open, spanning out eight or so feet at his sides.

The beauty of him stole Celestia's breath; the fear nearly took her to her knees. She stood firm, knowing the women beside her were filled with as much awe and trepidation as she.

"In the beginning," Sabian stated, "before the time of man, there was a great battle between those angels who believed in the One True God and those who did not. At the battle's end, those who did not believe were damned by the Creator, destined to a life in the pits of despair with the leader of the revolt, the master of vanity—Satan.

"But there were those angels who realized their mistake immediately. Filled with regret and repentance, they begged an audience with the Creator, prostrating themselves as they asked His forgiveness, even if they remained damned for all eternity.

"The Creator looked upon those who had followed what was once His most beautiful angel into ruin. A God of mercy, since their repentance was sincere, He forgave all. A God of justice, He knew a price was still required. But instead of damning the repentant, God gave them a sentence of eternal life in service to Him, to clean up the wreckage He knew Satan would design.

"The Golden Throne Room, normally filled with the voices of pureness and light, fell into chaos and wonder as the verdict was trumpeted for all to hear. Those few angels who had repented would be known as *The Brethren*, sheathed in physical form, commissioned to reproduce, capable of magic. They were to become an elite army of Guardians who would watch over and protect the Creator's newest creation. Man.

"Now, these many generations later, Satan's son has risen to a power so deviant even Satan fears him. Natas, the ultimate spawn of evil, is masterminding the cataclysmic destruction of mankind to prove he is greater than his own father, greater than God Himself.

"With the battle for all mankind rapidly approaching, The Brethren are desperately seeking the destined mates the Creator designed just for them. These women, once the mating ritual has occurred, enhance The Brethren's powers, and become the vessels to reproduce the Creator's future warriors."

Sabian looked at Celestia, his eyes filled with regret. "You bled silver the other day in the barn. I was sent to find *you*, to return you to the one chosen for you."

She felt outside of her own body, and the world around her spun. There was no stopping it this time. Blackness claimed her, and she never felt herself hitting the ground.

****

Sabian couldn't rejoice in the restoration of his angelic supremacies nor that he was still there instead of having *never been*. Something had changed as he sped forward and lifted Celestia before her mother and aunts could move. The return of his speed, his *powers*, was surprising, given he'd again disobeyed commands. He held her close and returned to the place he'd been with just a thought, watching those he now knew had great power of their own. As a man he hadn't known; as an angel, he felt the power of each radiating at him impotently.

"Let her go!" Haven demanded, rushing forward.

Sabian stilled her with a thought, and she froze only feet before him. "You cannot stop me. You will only bring harm to yourself if you try." He watched as Celestia's mother struggled and sighed when she gave up the fight with a cry of anguish. "I will release you, but you cannot come closer."

Tears streamed from her eyes as she stumbled back. Her sisters ran forward to capture her in their arms. "Please," she begged. "Don't do this! She's my baby!"

Sabian didn't expect to feel this bombardment of sympathy, not now that he was once again himself. He held Celestia to his chest, knowing he had no choice but what he was about to do, even as his heart broke. "I'm so sorry," he said with a strangled cry and willed himself into the heavens.

He landed, the firm footing an invisible stand. Before him stood Michael, and he bowed instantly, still cradling Celestia in his arms.

"You never seem to learn," were the first words radiating from Michael.

Sabian kept his head lowered in respect, in fear. He'd never had the honor of meeting the highest angel, nor was he sure he was happy to now. "I apologize sincerely, Archangel. I come to beg forgiveness and mercy."

"Rise, and look upon me."

Sabian stood slowly and forced himself to look upon he who would undoubtedly determine the fate of not only Sabian, but the Cavanaugh women as well. He trembled, unable to stop himself.

"What have you to say for yourself?"

This was it. His only chance. "I come to offer my existence in exchange for mercy for this woman and for her cousin, whom I was sent to slay."

"You feel it an equal exchange?"

Sabian shook his head. "No. I am not worthy of the ground she walks upon. This is why I seek mercy."

"You believe her to be of value to us?"

Sabian frowned, knowing Michael already knew the answer. "She is of the silver blood, one who is meant to belong to *The Brotherhood of the Fallen*. I am begging for Celestia to be released from that fate. As well as for the life of her cousin, whose soul I lost. She carries children. To take her would be to take them as well."

Michael smiled. "You are mistaken about this one. She is of no value to the Brethren. Her blood is that of magic and nothing more. Celestia will have great value upon the earth but is not one of the immortals sought."

Relief nearly took Sabian to his knees again and brought questions he knew he had no right to ask. But he had to. If not for himself, for them. "She will be returned safely to her family?"

"She will."

He didn't know he could produce tears in his natural form, but the respite allowed them to form and fall unchecked. "I humbly thank you. But what of she whom I failed to deliver?"

"Diamond is to be spared. She was always to be. If her earthly life was meant to end, no power on earth could have prevented it, not even that of the Cavanaugh women. This was all a test for you and had nothing to do with her. We sent you to Celestia because her silver blood would make you believe you were on Mission. Sending Bevolt, the angel who visited, was to reaffirm her position in your eyes. This was nothing but a test for you, Sabian. Nothing more and nothing less."

Sabian fell to his knees again, holding Celestia's limp body so tightly he feared he might crush her, but he couldn't help himself. These last few seconds with her were all he had. All he would ever have.

"And I have failed miserably." He kissed Celestia's forehead, then her lax lips, before placing her gently on the air holding them aloft. Sabian rose and looked again upon the one who would end him. "Please thank The Creator for giving me this time with her. It was worth losing my existence… It was worth everything."

Michael ignored his words. "Sabian, former Reaper of the Dead, you are again given two choices. You have learned compassion, sacrifice, and love. Three things you lost over the centuries while taking souls. Now that you have *succeeded* in finding them again, you may return to your place as soul transporter. *Or*, you may become human, and, if she will still have you, spend a mortal lifespan with the woman you love."

****

Returned to the human form, Sabian stood once again before the three women who looked at him in both relief and awe. Haven rushed forward, touched her daughter's hair and placed frantic kisses upon her brow. Celestia's eyes opened, and she struggled until Sabian knew he had no choice but to release her to her mother's care.

The aunts approached and helped Haven take a stumbling Celestia away several feet before they faced him with questions in their eyes. He looked at his hands, his arms, and then down his form and smiled.

"I am human. I am at your mercy. And I love your child so much I have given up eternity. What say you?"

Haven held Celestia close, but she looked at him with joy, before Rayne removed her hand from her niece and moved toward him, fear still tightening her eyes.

"What of my child? What of Diamond?"

Sabian held out his hand, and Rayne belatedly placed hers in it. "She is spared as well."

His own eyes filled with tears to match those of the powerful women around him, and he struggled to maintain his composure. He released her hand and slowly approached Celestia, knowing he'd have to find if all was for naught. He kneeled at her feet and looked up, hoping against hope she could find a way to forgive him.

"I love you. I will give my life to you and for you if you will have me. And even if you won't, I will protect you from afar all the days of my now mortal life."

Celestia gasped and moved forward, to place her hands on his face. "I can and I do, because now I have the power to read your truly human heart. I love you, too, Sabian, former reaper of the dead. And I'm so glad you once again look like the man I fell in love with. Your angelic form was beautiful and amazing, but all I need is the man." She lowered a hand and tapped his chest. "This man."

Sabian rose, and took her into his arms. He studied her

upturned face as if memorizing every inch. "That's good. Because that's all I'll ever be. A man. A mortal. Fallible, I'm sure, in many ways."

Celestia inhaled deeply, as her gaze held his. "Most importantly, you are forever mine, as I am forever yours."

Sabian nodded, embracing the promise, knowing the connection between them went far beyond physical need. Although hard to do, he finally broke their visual link, to smile at the older women silently witnessing what was the most important event of his long existence. Haven, Rayne and Destiny stood as a united force, holding each other's hands, tearful smiles on their identical faces. "I will love, honor and cherish Celestia for all the days of our lives. And I offer myself as your family's protection, whenever, and in whatever way needed."

With nothing more than a nod from each, the three matriarchs turned into mist and floated away. Sabian, chuckled, knowing he'd have to get used to living with a family of mystics, as a human, and he couldn't wait to start.

Beginning with the angel in his arms.

THE END

Dear Readers,

Thank you for reading *Celestial Liaison*, book eight of the Cavanaugh series! I hope you enjoyed this book! There are still four more Cavanaugh stories to come before the last story, *Gavin's Ghost!* The horror Gavin White lived through as a child in Mystic Waters has come back to haunt him as an adult. Only this is no ghost. This is the man who took everything from him as a child. Now Gavin has lost everything again, for very different reasons. The last thing he needs is trouble when he moves back to Mystic Waters for his family's help, but... *But*, that's a story for another day! ;)

While you await the next Cavanaugh release, I would like to introduce you to a *Celestial Liaison* **spin-off** series called the **Blood Moon Chronicles**. As you learned in Celestia's story, there are dangers ahead for the earth's occupants, and the sons of the repentant angels must find their destined mates quickly and at all cost! Or the earth will be lost.

Blood Moon Rising is available now!

The Cavanaugh Series

(The Cavanaugh Sisters Trilogy)
#1 **Mystic Thunder**
#2 **Touch of Lightning**
#3 **Tempest's Embrace**

(The Cavanaugh Series continues!)
#4 **Jewel of the Nile**
#5 **Sapphire Blues**
#6 **Diamond in the Rough**
#7 **Luna's Landing**
#8 **Celestial Liaison**
#9 **Zeus:** *Unbound!*
#10 **Apollo:** *Unleashed!*

Heracles: Undone (Not yet available)
Soleli's Secret (Not yet available)
Gavin's Ghosts (Not yet available)

The Blood Moon Chronicles
#1 **Blood Moon Rising**
#2 Blood Moon Waning (Not yet available)
#3 Blood Moon Falling (Not yet available)

Visit my website: **www.jcwardon.com**
Facebook pages: **www.facebook.com/jc.wardon** and
https://www.facebook.com/JCWardonNovelist
Tweet me: @jc_wardon.

Thanks for sharing my world. I'd love to hear from you!

JC Wardon

And… if you'd like a little taste of Apollo: *Unleashed!*… check out the following pages!

Apollo: *Unleashed!*

Chapter One

Apollo Cavanaugh-Whitehawk swung the hatchet, slicing deep into the short length of wood he'd cut from the much longer log of a downed tree. He bent down to lift the two pieces and threw them over where he'd soon stack the building pile. He'd been at it all morning, knowing there was no hurry to prepare for the still distant upcoming winter, but it was something to do now that he had so much time on his hands.

The subtle breeze blowing through the tress shifted and the sweetness of Mystic Mountain altered and took on an injurious smell. He halted in the process of lifting another cord to chop and tilted his face upward, lifting his nose toward the pristine sky, surprised and a little befuddled by the odd smell. Though the massive pines around his cabin blocked out a good deal of the sun's light, enough beamed through in the small clearing to reveal both a cloudless sky and the a hint of dark gray smoke which was now sucking at his lungs. A chill went up his sweaty spine and hardened the nipples on his equally glistening chest.

There a moment of hesitation, but only that, before he took off in the direction of the increasingly thickening smoke. He hadn't brought his cell phone out to the cabin, which was useless anyway on the mountain, but it had a built-in walky-talky feature that worked just fine and always alerted him when any kind of emergency broke out in Mystic Waters. He hadn't meant to leave it behind at the station, or that's what he been telling himself since seeking the solitude of his isolated cabin. He was on an official vacation for the next two weeks from the search and rescue unit of their fire department, because he needed to take a break.

A real one.

Where no one and nothing touched him.

The quiet mountain was becoming a hotbed of disasters, and his job was taking a toll.

Now he was forced to change his plans for an afternoon filled with reassessing his life, cold beers and hard work, to see what kind of trouble someone was in. He had no idea how far up the mountain he'd be required to run, so he did something he'd avoided for the past several years. Apollo called on the speed of the wind, which had been his mystical gift since the *ascending* when he was fifteen years old. His booted feet barely touched the rough terrain and tangling vegetation now as he sped toward the smoke with nearly sonic speed. Since it took only seconds to reach the burning car, he had to stop abruptly and, just as quickly, assess the situation.

A young woman hung upside down in the overturned burning car, her frantic screams and pounding on the glass making getting her to safety his first priority. Apollo placed his hand over his face and threw himself down on his stomach where he landed just beside the crushed driver's door. She looked at him with wide, terrified green eyes.

"Help me! Please!"

Apollo nodded. "Turn your face away!"

She did so immediately, and with one hard fist to the window, the safety glass cracked and gave. He pulled the pieces away, and looked inside as she turned back to him. "I'll get you. Just hold on!"

She nodded quickly, and he knew it was with hope more than assurance. He reached inside and fumbled with the latch of her belt buckle, until he found the button. He looked into her eyes, hoping the urgency within him wasn't reflected in his eyes for her to see. "I'm going to release your seatbelt and pull you out as you fall. I need you be completely limp and trust me."

"Do it!" she screamed and then coughed harshly.

The weight of her on his arm was welcome, though he feared he was hurting her as he pulled her out with haste. Once she was free of the seatbelt, which momentarily captured her right foot, he dragged her away, debating whether or not to lift her into his arms. All of his training said not to move such a victim, but he had no choice. The flames were getting bigger, and he was afraid the little sports car was about to explode.

"I'm sorry if I hurt you!" he shouted, when the flames turned to rolling roars. He lifted her with ease and sprinted backward away from the car. He got nearly twenty feet before the explosion came, throwing metal and burning fiberglass their way. He turned away from the flying debris and lowered her to the ground so he could cover her body with his own.

She said nothing and did not move. Apollo was afraid he might have broken something within her the wreck hadn't. He placed her flat on her back and listened through the top of the simple cotton dress as best he could for a heartbeat and felt for any signs of breath. It was a relief to see her chest expand suddenly and to hear the coughing that followed. Apollo looked into eyes that finally opened, and he breathed a sigh of relief.

"I'm trained to help you. Can you tell me your name?"

She coughed again, violently, eventually shaking her

head slowly. Though that was disappointing, it was a relief she could move her head and not react in pain. His training had apparently deserted him. He should have secured her head and neck and demanded she lie still until he could find a way to get help.

She needed x-rays and possibly a CAT scan to determine if there was internal damage, though her lifting her arms and grabbing him with such strength likely negated an upper spinal injury. Unless adrenaline alone was holding her together.

"Get me away from here, please!"

"I can't until I'm sure you can be moved."

She shook her head, tears filling her eyes. "I'm fine. Nothing hurts *too* badly, but it hurts, so I know I can move."

"It's too dangerous," he countered, "Someone will see the smoke and come soon."

"No! We have to go now. The men who were following me and bumped my car will come back to make sure I'm dead. Please, get me out of here now!"

Apollo was too stunned to react, giving her the opportunity to roll out of his grip. He watched in disbelief as she jumped to her feet and started to run. He hadn't realized how close to the mountainous road they were until just then. He glanced back to see the fire in the trees and brush and telepathed a message to his father, hoping that rusty skill still worked. He wished he could do the same with his mother, but Tom Whitehawk would have Mother Mountain take care of herself, and once everyone else connected in the ways that they did, his mother and aunts would handle the fires quickly, cleansing and restoring the earth in a way no one would ever know an accident had happened.

He turned and took off at a run, catching up with the woman as she stumbled her way over roots, vines and rocks. He pulled her to a stop and forced her to face him.

"Who are you running from?"

She tried to pull free, but Apollo held her still. "Answer me. Who is trying to kill you?"

She licked her lips and looked behind him in fear. When her gaze landed upon him again, there was resignation in the rise and fall of her shoulders.

"Men who want me or want me dead. I can't say more. *Please!* We have to go. If they find you with me, they'll kill you too."

He wanted answers but knew they'd have to wait. With surprising strength, she struggled against him again. He was afraid she'd really hurt herself if he didn't do as she asked. "I'll carry you. I just need you to hold on, and close your eyes."

Indecision held her immobile before she nodded quickly and allowed him to lift her. Apollo waited until she did as told, and he took off at a fast run. As much as he wanted to pull upon the power of the wind again, he knew he'd have to rely on only athletic ability. Otherwise, he'd have to explain the unexplainable.

It took ten times longer to return to his cabin than it had to get to the disaster, but even that was faster than made sense to most people. He set her on her feet at his front door and quickly ushered her inside.

"Where am I?"

Apollo closed the door behind him, and turned to face her. "You're at my cabin."

"No, I mean, where am I? On a map."

He frowned. "Mystic Waters. West Virginia. Mystic Mountain, specifically. You didn't know?"

She shook her head and glanced around the room. "Your place is nice, but I have to get away from here. When they find the car, they'll find me."

"No. They won't."

The panic was returning, settling in her eyes.

"*Yes*, they will. We're too close. I have to go. Please!"

It took a moment of debate, but Apollo decided to tell her what little he could. "Your car, or what's left of it, is miles away down the mountain. No one will know where you are."

Shaking her head, she looked at him as if he was crazy.

"There's no way that's possible. We can't be that far away."

Apollo smiled, hoping it reassured. "We are. I can run very fast. I'll ask again, what's your name?"

Indecision was in her eyes, and flight, her stance. Apollo knew she was scared, and he was pushing, even if gently. "I don't care who you are, but I have to call you something."

She nodded with jerky movements. "Isabella."

"Okay, Isabella, you're safe here. I live deep in the forest. There is only one way to get to my cabin by automobile, and that's only if you know where to find the turn from the road, and it's camouflaged and not readily noticeable. No one but my family knows there is a cabin here."

The relief he expected to see wasn't there. If anything, she looked more concerned.

"Why would you live in such isolation?"

Apollo moved toward the kitchen and, as expected, she followed. "Do you need some water?"

Isabella nodded and stood back as he retrieved two of the bottles his cousins manufactured in the town below from the waterfalls of Mystic Mountain. Being a native son alone was a perk in Mystic Waters. His father's people were generously blessed with magic and were one with the land. And the magical land, in turn, was one with them. These waters replenished *all* who drank them, but for his mystically infused Indian blood and the multi-cultural mystical blood of his mother's ancestors, the water offered even more.

She took a drink as he did, and they sighed together after swallowing. Zeus smiled at her, and she back at him. Something within him shifted. He looked away and settled his bottle on the counter. "To answer your question, I like solitude when I'm not working."

She took another drink, and he could see its properties were settling within her. She was more relaxed, and the fear eased from her eyes. She seemed more curious than anxious now, as she glanced around. The kitchen and living room were one, with only the sofa separating them. The single bedroom was off to the right, and the bathroom took up the left wing. Both were as wide as the living room/kitchen as they held equal importance. The bedroom also accommodated the small office he'd set up. The bathroom, as were all the bathrooms his family designed, was fully tiled and held a shower that was a room itself, a sauna he rarely used unless to thaw his body after being out working for too many hours in frigid winter weather, and a plain white toilet, which he was meticulous about cleaning.

He wasn't a germaphobe like some in his family, but he had high standards when it came to hygiene. And he could use a shower now. He looked over at Isabella and gauged her, relieved he had a little of his mother's ability to read people. She seemed content for the moment, but he still hadn't checked her out.

"Do you hurt anywhere?"

Isabella's glance flew his way, and her cheeks heated, as if she'd been caught snooping. He grinned, thinking her cute.

"Just a little. But nothing to worry about. I actually feel pretty great, given the circumstances. But I need to get this smoke smell off me. I just don't have anything to change into." She crossed to the large window at the front of the cabin and looked out.

"You don't need to worry about anyone coming. I would know if they did."

She turned and lifted a brow at him. "You have a security system?"

Hoping the minute hesitation went unnoticed, Apollo nodded. His security system consisted of strong intuition and Lycanthrope, who would soon come to guard the area. His cousin Sapphire and her husband, the Lycanthrope Alpha, made sure their pack didn't let harm come to any under the Cavanaugh protection. And this woman, whoever she was, was now under his.

"I have clothes that will be too big for you, but you can shower and change into them until we can wash your dress. And I have female cousins who will bring some. They are all about your size, give or take." Apollo cringed. He had no idea if they were or not. Figuring it didn't matter, he shrugged.

Isabella bit her bottom lip, something he found endearing. His mother did that when she was working out a problem in her head, and he figured his new guest was doing the same.

"I'd love the shower and your clothes. But I don't want anyone else to know I'm here...for however long I'll be here."

The worried look returned before she looked down at the floor.

"I have no idea where I'll go."

"You have time to figure that out. And you don't have to worry about my family. We protect people. They won't be rude and ask questions, at least not to you. If they ask me anything, I'll tell them to mind their own business." He grinned. "Nicely, of course.

"They won't say anything to anyone."

He'd almost told her they kept to themselves for the

most part, outside of work, but he didn't want her to fear she'd stumbled into a creepy family of inbred hillbillies. He certainly couldn't tell her they did so to protect themselves, and each other, from discovery. There were those out there who sought people who held magic, and their purposes weren't always pure. The safest thing for everyone involved was to keep their magic to themselves.

"Come on into my bedroom, and we'll see what we can find. Then you can hit the shower, and I'll get one after."

She nodded and followed him, stopping just inside the large room. He went on to the dresser, giving her time to access her situation at her own pace. He knew the subject of sleeping arrangements would come up eventually, so he figured he'd give her a break and go on and get it out of the way.

"The sofa turns into a full size bed."

He pulled out a T-shirt and shorts, thinking them her best bet. When he turned to her again, she was looking at him with tears teasing her lower lids. "Are you okay?"

She nodded and wiped at her eyes, leaving a streak of moisture across her cheek. "You're so nice. I don't know what to expect. But thank you for all this."

He didn't expect to feel uncomfortable, but her gratitude was humbling. He shrugged. "It's nothing."

Her lips, trembling, lifted. "It's not nothing, right now, for me, it's *everything*. I'm without a home. Without any means to help myself. And I don't dare try to find either, even if I knew how to...."

Apollo wanted to ask questions, but there was time. She needed to trust him first, he understood that, and he had it to give. "I'm on vacation from work for the next couple of weeks. I'd be happy to help you, in any way you need. All you have to do it tell me what that is."

Isabella's eyes closed briefly, before she looked to him

with confusion. "You're on... *vacation?*" She was very still for a moment, and then frowned as she looked around the room. "I'm sorry... I think that means I'm messing up your plans."

He found it odd that she made *vacation* sound as if he'd spoken it in a language foreign to her, but she was obviously traumatized by the wreck and whatever had preceded it. Apollo hoped to offer reassurance. "No plans. Just time off. You're actually keeping me from making busywork just to occupy my time."

She blew out a breath. "Are you sure?" At his nod, she reached out to take the clothing from his hands. Their fingers touched in the exchange, and their eyes met in surprise.

Apollo studied the sunburst fanning out from the center of her violet irises and found himself mesmerized and then a little drunk of a sudden. He was *certain* they'd been green before, but he had been in a panic to get her out of the car and must have made an error.

But he didn't think so....

Not wanting her to know he felt as if the earth had shifted beneath his feet, Apollo bit back questions about before, and focused on the now. "I've never seen eyes the color of yours."

She blinked rapidly before lowered her eyelids, making long black lashes fan out to cover her eyes. Apollo tried not to take it personally. He was sure that was not her intent. But the lost connection was another indication of her mistrust. He took a step back.

"I'll show you the bathroom."

He turned away, only to be stopped by her squeaky words.

"I'm special!"

He turned back and looked her over. She was young and amazingly beautiful, but he didn't know what she meant by *special*. "In what way?"

The fear was back in full force, and those eyes he'd studied now changed colors to a brighter green than the green of before. He blinked but didn't react outwardly otherwise, although his insides were humming with an excitement he couldn't explain. He reached out to her without thinking, and she stepped back.

Apollo lowered his hand. "What are you?"

Her lips pressed together, and then she shrugged. "I'm not sure, exactly. I've been captive all my life. A science experiment...."

ABOUT JC WARDON

JC Wardon loves writing fantasy and spends her days weaving stories for those who love it as well. Though she has great appreciation for romances, a juicy and complicated plot is what she holds most dear. Danger, mystery, and magic are the life's blood for her Mystic Waters Books. She hopes you are captivated and stimulated, and your hearts become engaged.

If you enjoyed *Celestial Liaisons,* please consider telling others, and writing a review.

WWW.JCWARDON.COM